THE CURSE OF ORILON

A REALMS OF ELSWYTH STANDALONE

WILLOW ASTERIA

Content Warning

Please be advised that this book may not be suitable for all audiences.

This book contains sexual content, kidnapping, shadow bondage, death, attempted sexual assault, graphic violence, and other topics some readers may not find suitable.

Realms of Elswyth

In the land of Elswyth, six portals exist that lead to the fae realms.

Orilon. Irolyth. Alari. Aeros. Khaldon. Tarak.

ELSWYTH
THE HUMAN REALM
VARIA
ZAMORA
MAGLA
PENDRIL
CALDOR
PORTAL TO ANOTHER REALM

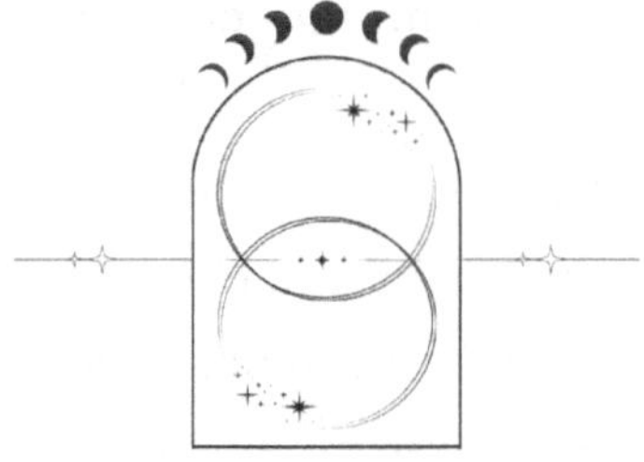

One

Days like today were my favorite. The apothecary wasn't too busy, but there was enough business to keep the day flowing smoothly. My aunt trusted me to run the shop alone while she made the deliveries to some of the more sickly and elderly clients.

As the only apothecary in the secluded town of Pendril, we were normally quite busy. However, for the past hour or so I didn't have a single customer. Using up my free time, I took inventory and made elixirs to keep our shelves full. With the change of the seasons, our tincture to soothe sore throats was running low. I was crushing some mint leaves when I heard the bell above the door chime, signaling someone was coming in.

"Good afternoon!" I said in a cheery voice before I looked up and saw who it was. "How can I help you today, Caden?" I said through clenched teeth. He was the last person I wanted to see today, especially alone.

He smirked as he adjusted the sleeve on his bright red shirt and approached the counter. Brushing back his light brown hair, he flashed a predatory grin as he leaned forward and rested his elbows on the glass countertop.

"You can help me by finally agreeing to be my wife," he said plainly.

I took a step back from the counter and crossed my arms angrily. Rolling my eyes at him, I replied with a huff. "As I have told you for years, I will never marry you."

Caden had been asking me to be his since we were teens. Now we were twenty-six, I was hoping he would move on, but unfortunately, that was not the case. He was not a very nice man. It was well known he would lie, cheat, and steal to get whatever he wanted. I had no interest in being his wife.

Anger contorted his face. "Amara, please be reasonable. You are almost thirty years old. Your timer is ticking."

I let out a chuckle under my breath. "Caden, we are the same age. If my timer is ticking, so is yours. Stop wasting your time on someone who hates you."

Caden's expression darkened. He stared at me for a moment with violence in his eyes. Before I could do anything else, he jumped over the counter and slammed me into the wooden wall in an instant. The shelf next to me rattled, and several of the jars crashed to the floor. His hand was wrapped around my throat to cut off my breath. I tried to push him away, but he grabbed my hands with his free one and held them above my head. He leaned in, towering over me, with a scowl on his face. His body was pressed against mine, pinning me fully to the wall.

"Amara, we live in a secluded town. There is no one else for you."

"Fuck you," I spat in his face.

He shook his head in shock and staggered back in surprise before anger flashed back to his face. "Oh, you little bitch. You will pay for that!"

The doorbell chimed, and my head snapped to the door. My aunt was walking in with a paper bag in hand. Caden quickly changed his demeanor as she cleared her throat.

"Hello, Caden. You know we do not allow customers behind the counter," she said in a firm tone. "I just saw your father at the market. He said he was looking for you. You better get home." Her eyes narrowed as she stepped closer to us.

"Yes, ma'am. I hope you have a lovely evening," he said with a warm smile before rushing to the exit.

I watched as he left, and the glass door shut. My hands trembled as I could still feel his fingers wrapped around my throat.

Glenda sat the bag on the counter and rushed over to me. "Oh, sweetie! Are you alright?"

I swallowed hard and nodded. "Yes, I am alright." My heart felt as if it was about to burst out of my chest. "Just a bit shaken, is all."

"Caden is a waste of air," Glenda said with a snarl. She walked over to the door, locked it, and flipped the open sign to 'closed'. "Next time he comes into the shop, make sure you have the dagger ready." She eyed the section of the counter where we had the mentioned dagger hidden. Luckily, we had never had to use it, and I hoped we never would need to.

In response, I nodded. To be honest, I was not sure I would have the strength to use it.

Glenda grabbed the bag and made her way up the stairs. The second floor of our shop was our two-bedroom home. I followed her upstairs and into the kitchen as she emptied the bag's contents onto the kitchen table and put them away.

"Other than your unfortunate run-in with that boy, I hope your day was ok. While I was out, I learned of two more fae attacks. A young couple snuck into the woods last night and were found dead this morning. Those poor dears, they were so young. Just last week, the Latoi family did not lock up on the new moon, and they did not survive the attack."

I couldn't help but shudder. The fae were horrid creatures that only came out at night and were the stuff of nightmares. Their skin was like snow and they had jagged teeth, long sharp claws, and large bat-like wings.

Every new moon they seemed to be the most violent and bloodthirsty. I heard of so many lives lost to the fae at this point, I was numb to it. We all were.

Deep in the forest that surrounded the town, there was a stone archway filled with purple mist. It was there long before the first settlers of Elswyth came to this mountain valley. This was where the fae came from, and was the only place in the entire country where any sort of magical beasts resided. We tried to build a wall around it, but every time we did, it would be destroyed within a few days. No one knew what was on the other side of the portal because any who passed through never returned.

It was a strict rule that no one was allowed in the forest at night, and many villagers gave themselves a curfew of dusk.

"I will pray to The Mother that they will find peace in the beyond," I said softly.

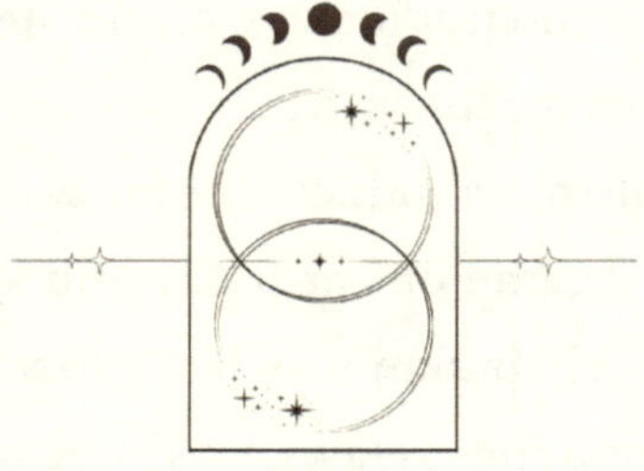

Two

One of my favorite things to do in this small town was meeting with my best friend every Wednesday night at Drago's, the local tavern, to discuss our latest reads we had gotten from the merchant that traveled through a few weeks ago. Jade and I were huge bookworms and had been since we were kids. We would constantly get into trouble in school for reading instead of paying attention to class.

Every week, we would sit in the same booth and watch as the bar filled with people. There were not many places for the locals to hang out in Pendril, so this tavern was always packed. It didn't hurt that they had amazing food and drinks. Jade and I shared a plate of nachos while we sipped on our drinks. If she had a good day, she would have a frozen cocktail with pineapple, coconuts, and strawberries. If it was a bad day, she had cinnamon whiskey, straight. Today was a good day.

I always drank the same thing, and the bartender, Sam, always had it ready for me as I was walking through the door. Sipping on my peach vodka cocktail, I listened as Jade went into detail about the morally grey hottie she was reading about in her dark romance. He was tall, dark, handsome, and very well-endowed. I had to grin because this week I read a vampire romance about a girl who was fated to be killed by her vampire mate. The man in that book was also very dark and handsome. I loved reading about men who were assholes, but I hated them in real life.

"Do you ever think you will leave this small town and travel across the mountains to find love?" Jade asked. Pendril was in a mountain valley, which is why it was so cut off from the rest of the country of Elswyth. Everyone who was born here lived in this town and would die here. We had very few visitors, the last ones being a family from Magla, who were traveling merchants.

Jade married her high school sweetheart, Jack, the Mayor's son, the day she turned eighteen. The two of them have been in love since grade school. I loved seeing my best friend happy.

In a town so small, pretty much all eligible candidates were taken by the age of twenty. I think the only man who was my age who wasn't married was Caden, and I would rather die a dusty old spinster than marry him.

"My duty is here," I sighed. "I will continue to learn the trade and take over as the town herbalist once Glenda retires." Of course, I would have loved to travel, but there was nothing I loved more than herbalism. It was the only thing that made me feel close to my mother.

My mother and Glenda were twins and were taught herbalism through their mother. For generations, the trade was passed down from woman to woman in my family. A part of me was sad, thinking it would end with me. Hopefully, I would get lucky, and a man from across the mountains would come and be the answer to my prayers. I wanted love, but I feared it would not be in the cards for me.

My parents were killed by the fae during a full moon attack when I was just a baby. Unfortunately, our home was set ablaze, and everything was lost. That fateful night, I was with my aunt and spared from the flame's wrath.

"You will be the greatest herbalist this town has ever seen," Jade smiled.

"Thank you!" I offered her a huge smile in return.

We went back to eating our nachos and talking about the books we wanted to read next. I dipped my cheese-covered chip into some sour cream as the tavern door opened. A group of men walked in, and the room filled with their loud and annoying voices. Already drunk, they stumbled and headed right to the bar.

"Seven shots of tequila." Caden's voice rang through my head, causing my body to tense.

Jade's head turned to me and raised an eyebrow. I started to tap my fingers against the table. My vision started to twist and turn as a pit grew in my stomach. Seeing Caden again so soon was not something I wanted to do. Especially with him drunk, who knows how he would react when he saw me.

"Amara, are you ok?" Jade's concerned voice snapped me back to the present.

I turned to her and gave her a nod, swallowing hard. "A headache just randomly popped up. I think I should probably head home."

"Oh, alright. I'm sorry you don't feel well. That hit you pretty fast." Worry filled her voice. "Do you want me to walk you home?"

"No, it's alright. It's not a long walk." My eyes never left Caden. I needed to know exactly where he was at all times. Luckily for me, he was too busy doing another round of shots, he hadn't looked this way.

She stared at me a moment before letting out a sigh and nodding. "Okay. Stay safe. It is almost dark."

I got up from the table and gave her my final goodbye with a hug. Making my way through the crowd, I tried to slip out of the tavern without Caden noticing me.

Once I was outside, I let out a breath of relief that he hadn't seen me. At this time of night, the town was already empty. So many people had already settled into their homes. The street lamps had already been lit for the night and filled the streets with an orange glow. I quickened my pace not wanting to be outside longer than I had to be. Even though it was not a new moon, that did not mean I was safe from the fae. Tonight, I also had another type of predator I needed to be even more afraid of.

The sooner I was home, the better.

Hearing the sound of heavy footsteps behind me, I quickly turned to see Caden and his friends. My eyes went wide as he stepped ahead of his group, and a devilish smirk took over his face.

"Hello, doll. It is time for your punishment, unless you have come to your senses and agreed to be mine," Caden purred.

"I will never be yours," I snarled at him.

"Then I can't protect you from what's going to happen next."

The men behind him fell into a full sprint, and my heart pounded in my chest as I turned and ran to make my escape. I turned down an alley, hoping to lose them in the maze between the townhomes. Blood pulsed in my ears the more I ran.

They screamed and called after me. Their voices filled my head with all the vile things they were going to do to me. As I kept up the breakneck pace, my breath got heavy, my vision tunneled, and a stitch grew in my side. I felt myself losing momentum. I was in no shape to be running through the streets of Pendril. Despite every attempt to keep my speed up, a strong hand grabbed my hair and yanked.

I fell backward and into the arms of one of Caden's friends, Amos. He wrapped his arms around me and held me in place. Screaming to be released, I squirmed and kicked. It wasn't long before Caden walked forward and stood in front of me. Seemingly unbothered from the run, he gently picked up one of my blonde ringlets.

"Oh, doll. You're definitely going to get what you deserve."

Just as he went to grab for my shirt the air filled with an ear-piercing screech. My heart skipped a beat, and my ears felt as if they were bleeding from the sound. Everyone's heads snapped in the direction of the scream.

Twenty feet away stood three fae.

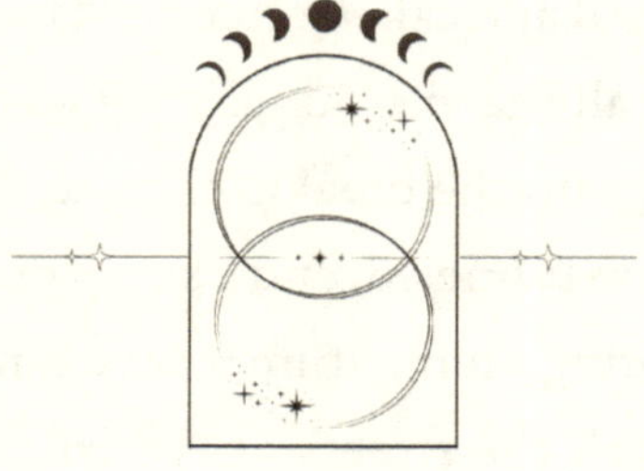

Three

Amos dropped me and ran off. Quickly, I scrambled to get back onto my feet. The fae rushed us, and their battle cries filled my ears. Their long claws tore through one of Caden's friends. His blood-curdling screams echoed off the brick homes as he was ripped to shreds. I watched in horror as the fae bit into his neck and ripped out his heart with its claws.

Bile rose in my throat. Never had I seen the fae in person, nor had I experienced such violence. My body quivered as I stood there frozen. A fourth fae joined the attack and pounced on Caden as he tried to escape. He fell onto his back, as the fae flared his bat-like wings and tore into his chest, feasting on Caden's flesh. More fae came into view, and their blood-red eyes locked onto us.

In my mind, I screamed at myself to run. It was what I needed to free myself from my paralyzing fear. I turned and ran as fast as I could as I caught my second wind. Sprinting through town, I screamed for the town guard, and almost immediately two came rushing toward me.

I finally stopped running, and I placed my hands on my knees as I tried to catch my breath. Finally, I forced the word out of my throat.

"Fae."

Falling to my knees, the contents of my stomach spilled onto the ground. I watched as their feet left my vision, and I heard the town's alarm begin to sound. One of the guards stepped back in front of me and helped me to my feet.

"Rush home and secure your doors," he said to me as more guards flooded the streets.

I nodded and collected myself. Quickly, I made my way back home. Chaos filled the streets as the guards sped past me and the screeches of the fae filled the air. I slammed the door of the apothecary shut behind me and locked it.

"Oh, Amara!" Glenda's terrified voice called from behind me. I turned and saw her standing on the stairs, in her pink wool robe, worry all over her face and tears welled in her eyes. "I am so glad you are alright! I heard the sirens and thought the worst!" She pulled me into a hug and held me close.

"I... I am ok..." I whimpered, still reeling from everything that had happened since I left the tavern. "I saw them... up close." I steadied my breath.

"Let's get down to the basement. It is safest there." Glenda grabbed my arm and guided me to the basement door. She opened it and ushered me in first, allowing me to descend the cement stairs as she locked and barricaded the door. Lighting a lantern, the small space illuminated. Wooden boxes were stacked against the wall, keeping the room neat. Opening the chest that stored our supplies for lock-ins, I grabbed our sleeping bags and set them up on the floor.

All we had to do was wait for the sun to rise and this nightmare would end.

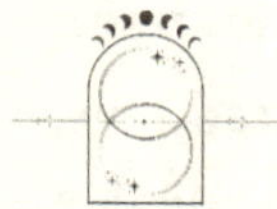

Unfortunately, by the time the alarm sounded, it was too late. Many people did not have enough time to secure their homes before the fae overwhelmed the town.

The next day was pure chaos. This attack was one of the worst the village had ever seen. Never had the fae gone that deep into town. The fae I encountered were not the only ones to invade. Other groups also came from the east and west. Over thirty fae in total attacked.

Glenda and I spent all morning making salves and elixirs to help heal the injured. The two of us had a system where I would gather and muddle ingredients and she would combine them into the proper potions. As we made them, the village healers and our regular customers took them just as quickly.

We were so busy throughout the day we did not have much time to talk about anything other than work. In the afternoon, when it finally slowed, Glenda finally spoke.

"It was not a new moon last night. It is so strange that so many fae attacked."

"Makes me worry about the new moon that is right around the corner. If it was this bad last night, how much worse could it get?"

"Indeed, a cause for concern." Glenda turned and went to grab the jar of vitella flower pollen, an important ingredient used in healing salves. She opened the jar and sighed. "We only have enough for two more batches." Glenda took out a scoop of pollen, added it to her mortar, and mixed it in with the other ingredients.

The vitella flower was a rare plant only found deep within the forest. It was very difficult to harvest. If done incorrectly, you would damage the plant, and it would not produce seeds for the next year or re-bloom. I had been practicing for years to get it right. The last time I harvested, I did not damage a single flower.

"I will go and collect more in the morning," I said to her with a smile.

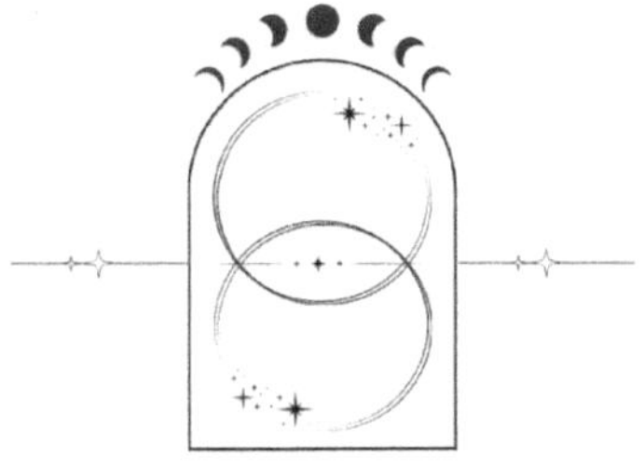

Four

I packed a small backpack full of harvesting equipment, water, and snacks the next morning and set out into the forest just after dawn. Throwing on my black cloak to fight off the autumn chill, I secured a dagger on the harness built into my cloak. The forest around Pendril was thick and filled with pines and firs, and the air smelled of fresh rain.

I traveled and searched for hours without any luck. My usual spots were bare, leaving me to go on a wild goose chase. The sun peeked through the canopy and illuminated the forest with a soft golden glow. The deeper in the forest I went, the more nervous I got. I did not want to get too close to the portal, but unable to find any vitella, I found myself heading in that direction.

After another hour of searching, I finally found a single flower placed in the center of a ring of mushrooms. Never had I seen anything like them. They were black-capped with a white stem. And a black, ink-like substance dripped from the gills. I would need to come another day to study these. There was no time to spare on side tasks today.

Stepping into the ring, I knelt before the plant and sat my backpack on the ground next to me. I pulled out my harvesting equipment and got to work. Luckily, there was a break in the canopy and it cast light down directly where I needed it to be so I could get a good look at the plant in the light. Using my tweezers, I opened the petals gently before sticking in my brush to pet the stoma delicately to release the pollen and trap it within the bristles.

The sound of a branch snapping caused my head to shoot up. Standing just on the other side of the mushrooms stood the most beautiful and terrifying man I had ever seen. Ice-blue eyes stared down at me with disdain. His hands were in the pockets of his black pants. My eyes went wide as my gaze rose to his wings. They were black as the void with golden flecks throughout that looked like the starry night sky.

"You are a long way from home, sunshine." His voice was like a smooth melody.

I hated how much I loved his voice. Everything around me darkened as if the sun focused all its rays on the very spot where I knelt. "Not too far. I spend much time in these woods." I pulled away from the plant with trembling hands, but I couldn't stand. My body wouldn't allow it.

The man chuckled as he pulled one of his hands out of his pocket and pushed back his long, white hair. Two thin braids with golden hoops framed his face. I could not stop staring at the black crescent moon, with the points facing up, tattooed on his forehead. Never had I seen anyone with such strange markings.

He knelt, so we met eye to eye. "Not enough to know you should never step into a fae circle, lest you be trapped."

His cold tone sent a shiver down my spine.

Fae circle? Was this man a fae? He did not look anything like the monsters I had grown so accustomed to seeing. What did he mean by trapped? Was I stuck here? I quickly reached for my dagger and pointed it at him as I finally stood, the paralyzing hold that was on me was now mysteriously gone.

"Stay back!" Slowly, I backed away. Something hard hit my back and my body tensed. Nothing should be there as before it was just air. I turned to see that I was now at the inner edge of the mushroom circle and a dark wall was now behind me, stopping my exit. It was as if the shadows transformed into this barrier. The dagger shook in my hand.

"I am not afraid of a tiny blade that you call a weapon," he chuckled as he stood and took a step into the circle. "All of you humans are the same. You come into the forest and take and take." Rage filled his voice.

Everything in me screamed for me to throw the dagger into his ice-blue eyes and run. My body betrayed me again and would not allow me to move a single muscle. He continued to step closer toward me. Pausing just before the flower, he looked down at it. His face softened and his gaze lifted back to me.

"Please," my voice shook. "Let me go."

As he took the final step to close the gap between us, I flung the dagger at him. All hope escaped me as he glided out of the way as if it was no issue. A deep laugh escaped his throat as he reached forward and grabbed my wrist, pulling me to him. I squirmed and tried to pull away, but his grip tightened, and his gaze dropped to my wrist, eyes widening in shock. Pulling my wrist up to his face, his gaze locked onto the eight-point star-shaped birthmark on my wrist. I attempted again to yank away.

"Let me go! Why are you doing this? Who are you?" I cried out.

He pulled me to him once again, wrapping his other arm around my waist, and held me against him.

In a faint whisper, he said, "The man who's going to marry you."

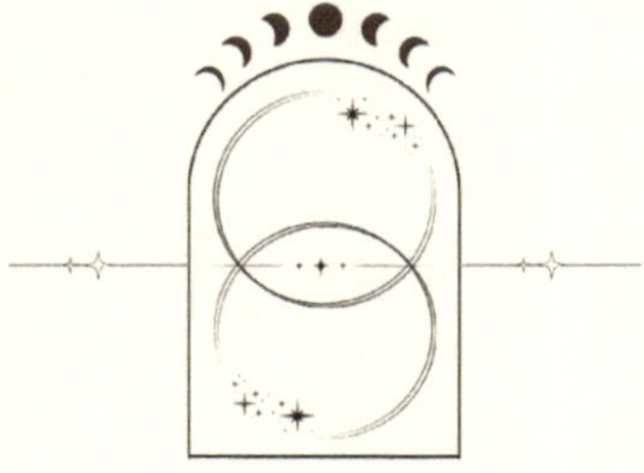

Five

I looked up at him and blinked hard. For a moment, I could not even articulate how I felt about his statement. Never did I expect anyone other than Caden to demand marriage from me. With him gone, I hoped I would be free. He held me closer, and the scent of bergamot and pepper filled my nose.

"I absolutely will not marry you! Release me at once," I demanded.

"Oh, you absolutely will, sunshine. Whether we like it or not." With a flap of his wings, we took to the sky.

Panic rose in me once again, and I now clung to him. My body trembled as I looked down at the world below us grow smaller and smaller.

"Please do not drop me!" I pleaded with him.

"I would never drop a woman as beautiful as you," he purred.

A faint purple mist filled the trees, and it snapped in my head exactly where we were going.

"No! No! Please not through the portal!" I screamed. "Please take me home!"

"I am." His voice was calm and collected.

Shadows filled my vision, and my eyes grew heavy. I found myself yawning, unable to fight back the sudden exhaustion I let sleep take me.

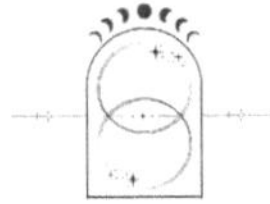

I couldn't open my eyes. Taking a deep breath, the warm scent of vanilla sugar encased me. Was everything that just happened a dream? The bed in which I laid felt much more comfortable than my own. I finally forced them open and shot up, the blankets piled around my waist. A new place surrounded me. The room was large and the bed was centered against the back wall. The walls were stone and bare.

Panic welled in my chest. To add to it, I realized I was now in a small black silk nightgown. Where were my clothes? Who put this on me?

On the left wall was a large window, and in desperation to know more about where I was, I jumped out of bed and rushed over to it. Looking down, I realized I was in a tower of a very large castle that sat on a plateau, surrounded by a few mountains. Beyond the mountains was a large forest. The castle was made of dark stone, but green moss and ivy had taken over many of the outer walls.

This forest was like nothing I had ever seen. The treetops were varying shades of blue, purple, and green. In the distance, I could see that undeniable shimmering purple mist of the portal as it clung to the treetops. Even if I could escape here, would I be able to traverse this forest to get to the portal? My heart broke as I realized how far away I was from the only thing that could return me home.

I turned toward the door and rushed over to it. Twisting and yanking the handle, I quickly learned the door was locked, and I was trapped. I banged on the solid oak door, pounding harder and harder with each knock, but it did not budge. I screamed for help. For anyone to release me.

To free me from my prison.

Hours passed, and my throat grew sore. I gave up. Turning back to the bed, I flung myself into the soft feather pillow, sobbing and screaming into it.

After what felt like many more hours, I heard the door open from behind me. I shot up and saw a young woman walking in with a cup of tea. She quickly shut the door behind her.

Her wings also looked nothing like the fae from back home, or like the wings of my kidnapper. They were light orange with a white border. Her alabaster skin was covered in freckles.

"Good morning!" Her voice was so cheerful. "My name is Poppy, and I will be your lady's maid during your stay. I made you some licorice and honey tea for your throat." She walked over to the side table and sat down the cup. Her fiery red braid fell to her front as she bent over. She looked back at me and gave me a warm smile.

"Are... you fae?" I finally spoke.

"Since the day I was born," she giggled. Her voice was light and bubbly. She sat down on the bed next to me.

"You don't look like a horrid monster. Where are your fangs? Your claws? Your eyes are bright amber, not blood red." I raised an eyebrow at her.

"I am not a vox! How dare you!" A look of anger took over her face. "I will let that one slide since you are from the human realm." Just as quickly as the anger came, it went. Her face was back into a soft smile.

Offending her was the last thing I wanted to do. Though she was fae and I did not trust her, Poppy seemed kind. "Vox?"

"Yes. The vox are fae who were cursed into turning into those horrid creatures. Bless their souls. No need to worry, here in the castle you are safe." Poppy stood back up and took a step toward the door.

"The vox are all we know back home. I never encountered an uncursed fae before the man in the woods."

"Welcome to Orilon," she giggled, "one of the fae realms. You can expand your knowledge of the fae tonight."

"Tonight?" I raised an eyebrow. Also, did she just say *one of the fae realms*? How many realms were there, and did others also have monsters like the vox?

"Oh yes. You are going to have dinner with the king." She clapped her hands together excitingly.

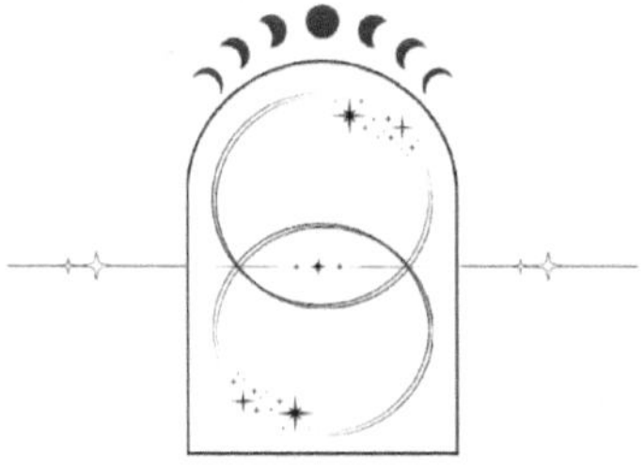

Six

For the first time in my life, I found myself being pampered. Back home, we could not afford luxuries like these. I hated I could easily find myself getting used to this. Poppy prepared me a warm bath, using a variety of exotic soaps. Once washed, she did my hair and make-up and dressed me in one of the most beautiful gowns I had ever seen. It was a dark blue satin fabric with a silver shimmer running throughout it. Once I was ready, she took me over to the full-length mirror with a golden frame.

My eyes welled with tears as I had never seen myself look so beautiful in my entire life. My fair skin was radiant from the cosmetics Poppy applied. My bright green eyes were accented by a golden shimmer on my eyelids.

My shoulder-length curly blonde hair was pulled back on both sides with golden clips.

"Come along. We do not want to be late," she said as she opened the door and waved for me to follow her. We walked through the halls of the dark stone castle. The floor was lined with a black rug with golden trim. Focusing hard, I studied every turn, every direction. I would take my time and plan out my escape.

Not once did I see any form of exit as we traveled the twisting hallways. Most of the doors were kept shut, leaving only my imagination to fill in the blanks. Finding my way out was going to be harder than I thought.

Once we reached the dining room, Poppy guided me to the end of the long table that was set for two, a place setting on each end.

"The king should be here shortly. Please sit," she said as she motioned to the chair.

"Are you not staying?" I questioned as I took my seat.

"Oh, no." She walked back toward the exit. "I have other things I must attend to. Enjoy dinner." With that, she left the dining room, leaving me alone.

Looking around, I once again took in as many details as I could about the space. There were two exits on the east and west walls. The far wall had a fireplace centered with a large black tapestry above it. Gold sparkled through it, matching the wings of the man who took me. Some of the gold spots appeared slightly larger than the rest and formed a geometric pattern.

I stood and walked over to it, examining it. When I looked over to the doorway I came through, I noticed there were no guards that I could see. Thinking back on it, I did not see anyone while Poppy was guiding me through the halls. How easy would it be for me to leave and escape? The better question was, how far would I make it dressed the way I was in an unknown forest?

Annoyance built in me as I continued to await the king's arrival. I decided I would stand by no longer. I had to take the chance and make my escape. I turned toward the door and took a step as a familiar dark and smooth voice came from behind me.

"Sorry for keeping you waiting. I had business to attend to."

I turned and saw the man who had kidnapped me. He wore a black suit with golden trim and buttons. His wings were neatly tucked behind him.

"Very rude of you to kidnap someone and then make them wait for you," I snarled.

He motioned for me to return to my seat, and I did. I understood the role I had to play for now. If I could get him to trust me, and think I would follow his commands, perhaps he would offer me some freedom. It would be then I would escape.

"I do not keep time based on humans," he growled. "I have more important things to worry about." He took his seat at the far end of the table. Leaning back in his chair, his facial expression cold, he lifted his right arm and snapped twice.

Servants filled the room and brought wine and food. I stared down at the broth-based soup and took in the scent of the herbs from the meatballs, spinach, and pasta that floated in it. It looked delicious and my stomach growled. But no matter how hungry I was, I would not eat this food. I was afraid it was enchanted or laced with some sort of poison. This was the same reason I avoided the tea Poppy had given me.

"No, thank you. I won't be eating."

"Yes, you will. I will force you if I need to. I can't have you die on me before I am done with you." He looked at me with contempt through his thick eyebrows as he sipped his wine. His ice-blue eyes pierced my soul with their intensity.

"Done with me?" My chest tightened as I fought against my rage and rising panic.

"Yes. As I told you before, you and I will wed. Then the curse will be broken, and then I can return you to the human realm." He set down his glass and leaned forward. "Take a bite now, or I will force-feed you," he snarled. Leaning forward, he watched me intensely.

I picked up the spoon and scooped up a meatball from the soup and ate it. It was so tender and juicy. Struggling to keep my composure, I nearly melted from how good it tasted. It was so amazing, I nearly had forgotten where I was and who was in my company.

I snapped back into the conversation. "I don't know what makes you think I could help you lift a curse among the fae."

"You're the chosen one. I have waited centuries for you." He shrugged his shoulders as if this was just an everyday occurrence for him.

"The chosen one?" Sitting down the spoon, I leaned back in my chair. My gaze fixed on the king.

"A story for another day." He waved his hand, dismissing me. "I hate humans, so this is not a walk in the park for me, either. We *will* be wed, and I *will* save my people." He snapped his fingers once again and the main course was served, only to me. "Enjoy your dinner. I will tell you when I have everything ready for our wedding." With that, he stood and vanished into shadows.

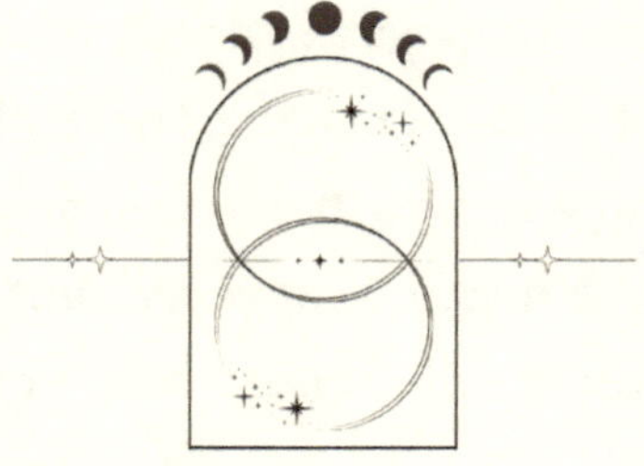

Seven

For the next two weeks, I stayed locked in my room. Poppy only allowed me to leave for dinner. She visited for only about an hour or so a day. When I woke up in the morning, breakfast was already sitting on the table by the window. She would stop by to deliver lunch and new books around noon. In the evening, she would take me to the dining room, disappear during dinner, then return me to my room. She refused to tell me anything about the king, the castle, or Orilon. According to her, the king would tell me everything I needed to know.

The king had not shown his face since our first dinner.

I hated being here, but being locked away and kept on a tight leash, I did not have any more of an idea of how I was going to escape. What type of psychopath kidnaps someone, tells them they are going to marry them, and then ignores them for two weeks?

Luckily for me, Poppy brought me tons of books to read, and with nothing else to do, I found myself reading one to two books a day. She also brought me a million articles of clothing. Never had I seen so many different fabrics, colors, and patterns in my entire life. She said the clothes I was wearing when I arrived did not fit my station here at the castle.

As the days went on, I found myself getting extremely lonely. It was getting harder and harder to get out of bed. My head was filled with thoughts of Pendril. Every night I found myself sobbing myself to sleep thinking of my aunt and Jade. I missed them so much. Did they think I was dead? After this much time, were they still looking for me, or did they think I was another victim of the 'fae'?

This morning, the sun shone through the window just right, covering the room in an iridescent rainbow. I sat up and stretched my arms above my head. Walking over to the table, I picked up the perfectly sweet coffee and took a sip. The scent of maple and butter filled my nose from the waffle that had been left for me for breakfast. I sat down and ate it, staring out the window, my gaze focused on the portal.

Once I was done eating, I made my way to the adjoining bathroom and took a shower. Lavender-scented steam filled the room. Once clean, I stepped out of the shower and dried off. As I ran the towel through my hair, a firm knock sounded at the bedroom door. I nearly jumped at the sound of it. I stayed in the bathroom, ignoring the knocking.

"It is me," he called out through the door. "May I come in?"

I wrapped the towel around me and walked over to the door. "No."

"Please," he growled.

"Fine," I sighed.

The door opened, and the king stepped inside. His gaze fell to me, and he choked on his breath. He quickly straightened his back and looked up at the ceiling. Clearing his throat, he finally spoke.

"Poppy told me it is bad to keep you trapped in here and you like to read. Please allow me to escort you to the library." He cleared his throat once again. "I will wait outside. Be ready in five minutes." With his final word, he turned on his heels, walked out, and shut the door behind him.

I giggled to myself. The thought of him being flustered brought me joy. I finished drying off and put on a simple blue dress. Excitement filled me. I could not deny I could not wait to get out of this room, even if it was with the man who kidnapped me.

I opened the door and stepped out. The king leaned against the wall with his arms crossed. All evidence of him being bothered was now gone.

"You look lovely, for a human," he said coldly. He kicked off the wall and took a step to close the gap between us. The citrus-spiced scent filled my nose as he lifted my chin so our gaze met.

"When you say it that way, it is not a compliment." My heart pounded in my chest.

He smirked down at me and then pulled away. The king walked down the hall and waved for me to follow him. "Come along, sunshine."

The nickname started to grow on me. It was one of the few things of light in this castle of darkness. My kidnapper and I walked the halls in silence for some time. His white hair floated behind him as he walked. Shadows clung at his fingertips. I watched as he squeezed his hand into a tight fist. The white of his knuckles showed through the shadows.

I had been so caught up in watching the king I stopped paying attention to the castle. I had absolutely no idea where we were. This section of the castle had some of the most beautiful paintings of the forest. I had never seen such gorgeous oil paintings. If I was not trapped here, I could see myself falling in love with the beauty of Orilon.

"What is your name?" He questioned, snapping my attention back to him.

"Why would I tell you my name? You have not told me yours."

A deep chuckle escaped his throat. "That is fair. My name is Ezra. Ezra Kincaid, the last King of Orilon." He continued walking, but never once did he look back at me as we spoke.

"The last?" I asked as I continued behind him.

"I am the last of my family's line. With the curse, there are not many fae left." He spoke in a distant tone. "The other realms have abandoned us. You, sunshine, are my last hope to save my kingdom."

"That is a lot to put on someone. How are you sure it is me? You don't even know my name!" The questions forced their way out of my throat.

Ezra turned toward me and stopped. I froze in my spot, my heart pounded as he slowly took a step toward me and said nothing as he closed the distance between us. I stepped back and felt something hard hit my back. I turned my head and saw a wall of shadow formed behind me, just as it had in the mushroom ring. I turned my head back toward Ezra, who was now directly in front of me. He lifted his arms and pressed his palms onto the shadow wall, trapping me between the wall and him.

Swallowing hard, I refused to break his gaze. A shiver ran down my spine as his power radiated from him. I did not want to be this man's enemy.

"What is your name, sunshine?" He snarled. His blue eyes pierced my soul. His tiny braids hung in between us.

"A.............. Amara."

"Amara what?" His gaze and tone did not falter

"Amara Smythe."

He smirked and pushed off the wall. The wall behind me vanished, and I stumbled back, but he reached out and caught me by my wrist to steady me. Once I was stable, he turned and continued to walk away. I stood there frozen. My heart pounded in my chest, and I could still feel the electrified air around me.

"Don't fall behind, Amara," Ezra called out to me. His voice pulled me out of my own head. My name on his tongue was intoxicating.

I rushed to catch up to him, and we entered a massive library. There were two levels with floor-to-ceiling bookshelves. In the center of the room sat several tables, with rows of shelves surrounding them. There was not a single empty shelf. There had to be more books in here than I could read in my entire life. My jaw dropped as I stepped past Ezra to get a better look at the library. Never in my life had I seen so many books. Ezra came around to my front.

"Poppy told me the type of books you like. They can be found over in section X. I will allow you to make your selection in private." He pointed over to the section of the library he mentioned. Heat rose to my cheeks, and that playful smirk returned to his angled face. "No need to blush. I understand now that we met you will think of me as you read them."

"Absolutely not!" Though he was handsome and charming, I would never think of him in that manner.

"Just keep telling yourself that, sunshine," he said as he winked.

I gave him a vulgar gesture, and he let out a deep chuckle.

"You seem to ask Poppy a lot about me," I said with a raised eyebrow as I studied his face.

"Of course." He sat down at one of the tables. "I told her to learn all she could about you so I did not have to waste my time doing so."

I rolled my eyes. Just like that, all the charm he had was thrown out the window. "You're an ass." Turning away from him, I made my way over to the section he told me about. Every romance author I ever heard of and more lined the shelves. With no idea where to start, I slid over the ladder, climbed it, and took the first book on the top shelf.

"You are free to come to the library whenever you please, but only the library. Call for Poppy and she will escort you. If you go anywhere but the library, you will be punished." His voice was right in my ear, but as I spun and looked around for him, he was nowhere near me. I got down off the ladder and walked back to the table he was sitting at.

Ezra was gone.

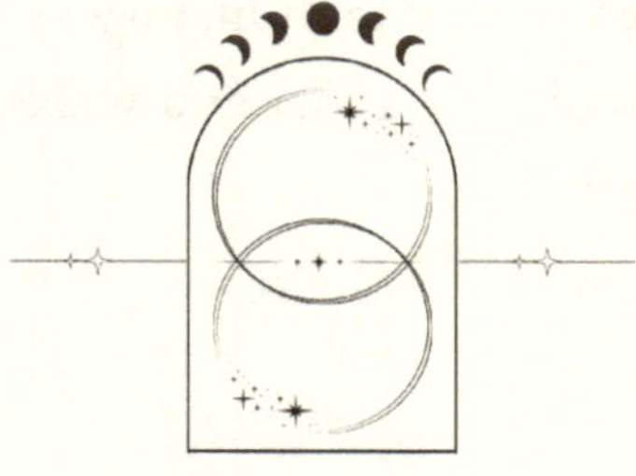

Eight

Over the next few days, I found myself spending every waking moment in the library. I discovered a tiny reading nook on the back wall with a window that overlooked the forest. The window seat had so many cushions I ended up removing some of them to make room for myself and my stack of books. There were more books than I could read in a lifetime. Spoiled for choice, I read them in the order they were arranged on the shelf. Gathering a small stack, I made my way to the reading nook.

Deep into my novel, I heard sounds of rustling papers and footsteps from deep within the library. I sat straight up and looked around. The noise stopped. "Poppy?" I called out. "Ezra?" I followed up when there was no response.

Maybe it was just my paranoia building that caused me to hear the noise. I brushed it off and went to read my book once again. It had just gotten to a very smutty scene that caused my core to melt when another noise pulled me out of the book once again. I shut my book and sat it down on the bench as I stood.

I tiptoed, following the sound of the rustling. Peering around a corner, I saw an older man stocking the shelves. His short silver hair matched the metallic gleam of his wings, and they both stood out against his dark complexion. He turned and his brown eyes met mine. He jumped, reaching for his chest.

"My Lady!" He gasped. "I am so sorry to disturb you! I will be done and gone in just a moment."

"No, it's ok! You don't need to go!" I exclaimed. "I just did not know anyone was here. The noise startled me."

"I am always here. I was ordered not to disturb you. The king did not want you to be afraid."

I raised an eyebrow at him. "Afraid? Of what?" Now that I thought about it, the only staff I had seen was Poppy and the servants at dinner. "Are there others who work in the castle?"

"Yes. He said you were afraid of the fae. There are a few of us left here in the castle. Unfortunately, many of the fae have been turned into the vox." He continued to stock the shelves with the books on his small metal cart. "My name is Gil. I am the royal archivist. It is a pleasure to meet you."

"It is nice to meet you as well." I offered a soft smile. "I feel bad you have had to work around me the past few days."

"It is no worry," he said with a shrug. "It truly is no issue. Please let me know if you need anything."

"Could you tell me how to leave the castle and go home?" I asked in a sarcastic tone. I knew it was a hopeless question.

"No," he let out a deep belly laugh. "The king would have my head. I understand he is hard to deal with. He has not been the same since he lost his family to the curse. Please know he has a good heart."

I leaned against the bookshelf and gnawed on my lip for a moment before speaking. "He lost his family?"

"Oh, yes. The royal family of Orilon all turned into vox about twenty years ago. Well, all except King Ezra, who was Prince Ezra at the time." Gil stopped stocking the books and sighed. "They had killed most of the castle staff before Ezra was able to cut them down." He choked on those last few words, and his eyes misted. "It was one of Orilon's darkest days."

"That sounds horrid," I whispered. Thinking about my own parents and how they, too, were claimed by the vox, I could not imagine what it would be like to have to hunt them down and stop them from killing more of the town of Pendril.

It seemed like the king and I had more in common than I thought. The vox had taken from us both.

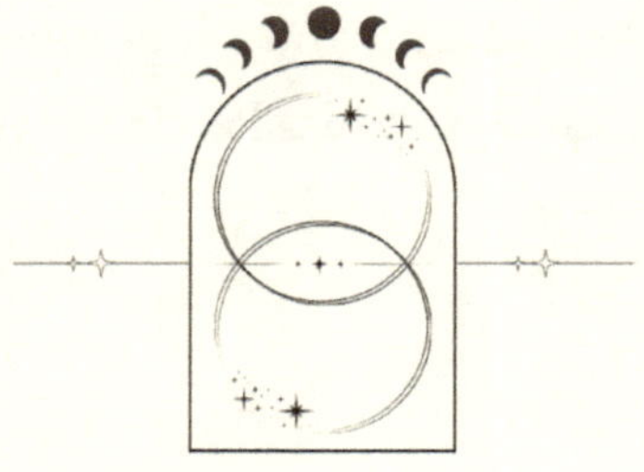

Nine

The next day, I sat at the table near the window in my room, sipping a cup of coffee. The mug pressed to my cheeks, and my eyes closed as I took in the sound of the rain. I had yet to make my way to the library for the day. It was one of those dark and dreary days that made you want to stay curled up in bed.

My eyes opened to a soft knock on the door. After calling out to see who it was, the door opened, and Poppy entered. She had a huge grin on her face.

"Good afternoon, Poppy." I smiled.

"Good morning! I hope you have had enough coffee this morning!" She motioned to the mug that was still pressed to my face. I nodded in response. "You are going to be full of energy for tonight! Wonderful!"

I narrowed my eyes at her warily. "Is something special happening tonight?"

"King Ezra requests you have dinner with him. He has things to discuss!"

"Good, because so do I."

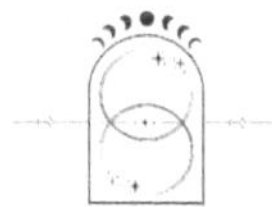

When we arrived at the dining room, Ezra was standing just past the entrance. He wore a black button-up shirt with the top few buttons loose and the sleeves rolled up just before his elbows. He was more casual than I had ever seen him.

"Good evening, Amara. It is time for us to discuss our wedding. Please sit, and I will have dinner served to us shortly." He gently took my arm and led me away from Poppy and to my seat. He even pulled my chair out for me. I looked at him with narrowed eyes as I sat, and he pushed in my chair. He made his way over to his seat, his white hair flowing behind him. Once sat, he snapped his fingers, and servants came out and served wine with a cheese soufflé. I watched as he sipped from his glass, his ice-blue eyes glued to me.

"Why did you tell your staff to hide from me?"

He stared at me through his brow and lowered his glass. "Gil told me the two of you met." He leaned forward. "I knew the fae made you uncomfortable. The situation is not ideal. I am just trying to make it easier for you."

"That is very kind," I said as I took a bite of the soufflé.

"Contrary to popular opinion, sunshine, I am a kind king."

I rolled my eyes and chuckled. "Sure, you are."

Ezra finally took a bite of his food and smirked at me. Shadows danced around him as if they begged for his attention. He sat down the fork and swallowed his bite, leaning back in his chair once again. "Our wedding will be held in two weeks. Poppy will get everything coordinated for you."

I hated the idea of marrying him, but at this point, escape seemed impossible. "And once we are wed, you will return me to my family?"

"Yes. I will take you back to the human realm." He took another sip of his wine. "For the next two weeks, each day you and I will spend one hour together, and we will have dinner together every night."

My eyes went wide. My heart pounded in my chest. I didn't want to be around him more than I had to be. A pit formed in my stomach. Ezra was terrifying to be around. His cold gaze stared down at me. I could sense his power and it threatened to devour me. I could not lie. I was also excited to spend more time with the King of Orilon.

"Why? I thought you did not want to be around me and you had better things to do." I raised an eyebrow.

"Oh, I do. I hate being around you," he said rolling his eyes. "There are many things I need to be doing and I would rather be doing." He leaned forward and rested his elbow on the table. Holding his head in his hand, he rubbed his temple with his thumb. "However, we need to convince the priestess we are in love."

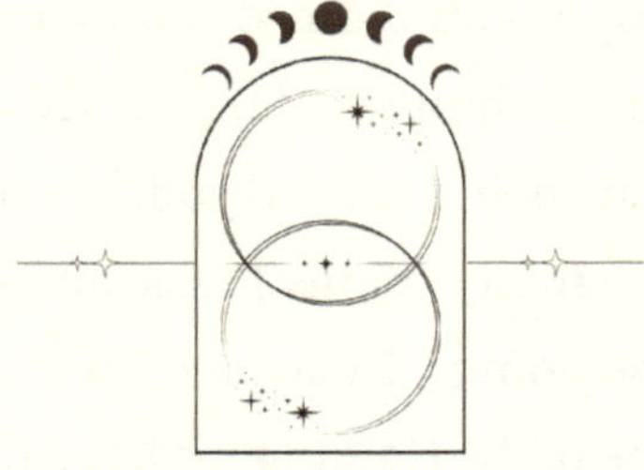

Ten

The next morning, Poppy barged into my room, and the sun hit her face just right, illuminating her golden eyes. She had a white sundress draped over her arm.

"Good morning!" She squealed. "The king requests your presence. He wants to give you a tour through the royal gardens."

"There are gardens?" I perked up, a large grin forming on my face.

"Oh, yes. I think you will love them."

I knew I would. As an herbalist, plants were one of my favorite interests. It was one of the hobbies my aunt and I shared. Thinking about all of the plants I kept back home in my room, I knew Glenda would take care of them until I returned. "Sounds wonderful."

"Great! Let's get you ready." She dressed me in the white sundress and pulled my hair back with a white ribbon. "You look wonderful!"

Poppy guided me to the greenhouse entrance, which was a large set of frosted glass doors. Ezra leaned against the opposite wall. His gaze was on the ceiling. He toyed with the golden hoops that were woven within the braids that framed his face. Once we got closer, he looked over at me and smiled.

"Thank you, Poppy!" He pushed off the wall and stepped over to us. "Are you ready, sunshine?" He looked down at me with a genuine smile.

Poppy gave me a little wave, then ran off.

"I am so excited! I love plants!" I giggled, not able to hide my enthusiasm.

"I could tell. I was shocked at how well you harvested vitella. Most cannot harvest it without damaging the plant. Only someone who truly cares for plants would be able to do that."

"My aunt taught me. I come from a long line of herbalists." Again, I felt my heart crack just a little as I spoke of home. I prayed to The Mother she was doing alright.

"Fascinating," he said as he opened the door to the gardens. Humidity hit me as we entered the large glass dome. I was awestruck by how many tropical plants there were. The gardens were filled with leaves and floral blooms in all shades of green, purple, pink, red, and orange.

As we walked the stone pathways, Ezra pointed out some of the rarer plants as well as some that were exclusive to Orilon. As he talked, I saw a blue glow emanating from one of the plants. It was absolutely enthralling. Ezra continued to walk, and while I heard the deep hum of his voice, I could not understand the words. I needed a closer look at the blue glow of the flower. I needed to be near it. A large blue flower bud was in the center of the glow.

The flower opened and revealed large sharp teeth. Vines shot from the ground and wrapped around my body. I wanted to squirm and fight, but my body would not allow me to move. The vines lifted me into the air and brought me closer to the flower.

Shadows darted from behind me and enveloped the plant. Before my eyes, the life was drained from the plant and the vines dropped me. Before I could compose myself, strong arms lifted me, and the bergamot and pepper scent filled my nose. Calm washed over me, and I leaned into him.

"Ezra," a soft whimper escaped my lips.

"Are you alright? I am so sorry, sunshine." His voice was filled with worry, his breathing was heavy, and I could feel his heart pounding in his chest as he held me close.

I looked up at him. "You're sorry?" He sat me down on my feet.

"Yes! There are not many gardeners left, they used to keep the plants in line. I thought all the carnivorous plants were removed ages ago. I should have been more careful. That one is known to lure humans in with their light. Once a human sees it, they are put in a trance and cannot escape. Did the vines hurt you?"

I shook my head in response. My entire body quivered in fear. Ezra took my hands in his to hold them steady. "What were those shadows?"

"I have shadow magic. I can control and manipulate the shadows around me. I can also use those shadows to drain life from anything. Do you want to return to your room? I would understand if so."

Somehow the thought of returning to my room felt like a worse choice even after being attacked by a plant. "No, I want to continue. Just keep me close," I said softly.

"Always." He wrapped his arm around me and continued the tour of the gardens.

Just last night he told me he hated me. I couldn't help but wonder if that was the truth. He was being so tender with me now. I saw the terror in his eyes after I had been attacked. That was not the look you gave to someone if you hated them.

He walked me over to a side door. "There are no other carnivorous plants in here. You will be safe." He opened the glass door and ushered me inside. This greenhouse was filled with a wide variety of orchids, all in bloom. They were truly divine. I took a step into the room and looked around at the flowers.

"Wow, they are all so beautiful," I said. I heard Ezra mumble something from behind me, and I turned to face him. "What was that?"

"Nothing." He brushed his hand through his hair to keep it out of his face as he looked away from me. "What do you want for dinner tonight? I realized I have always chosen. I don't even know what you like to eat."

"I like everything." I shrugged as I looked at a cattleya orchid with its bright orange flowers. "Everything we have eaten has been so delicious!"

"Perfect," he smirked. "I love surprising you, sunshine."

I was confused by his kindness, but maybe part of his strategy of convincing the priestess was just faking it constantly so that our love looked real when the time came. Still, I needed to be cautious and mind whatever games he was playing.

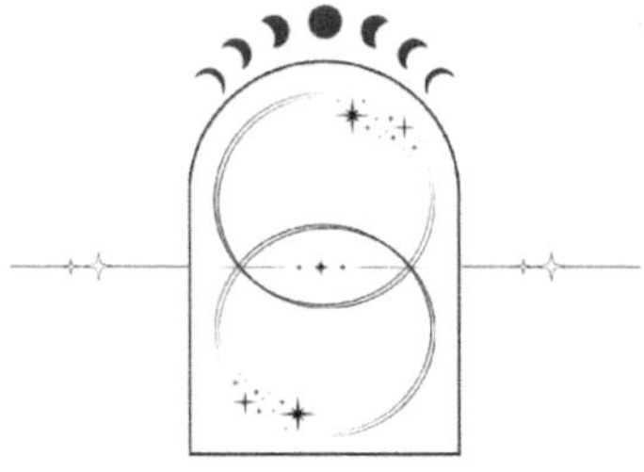

Eleven

Music filled the air, and it was light and romantic, and a calm washed over me as Poppy guided me to the dining room. It was as if all my worries washed away, I wasn't sure what caused this change in my mood. She had dressed me in a black satin dress with golden accessories. Long chain earrings dangled from my ears that matched the necklace that hung down my neck.

A shadow figure stood in the corner of the room, playing the violin, and I was mesmerized by the bow gliding across the strings.

"Have a good dinner," Poppy giggled as she left me alone in the dining room.

Waving goodbye, I let out a huff of air. Of course, Ezra was not yet here. Part of me was excited to see him, but I should not allow those feelings to exist.

The shadow figure lowered the violin and turned to me. "Please sit. I will be there in just a moment." Ezra's voice projected from the figure. I jumped from the shock of it, then took my seat, my eyes never left the figure. It played once again.

After a few moments, Ezra walked out with a bottle of wine in one hand and two glasses in the other. "Good evening. I'm sorry I am late." He sat the two glasses on the table next to me and popped the cork. "This is a sweet white from my family's vineyard." He filled both glasses, took his, and headed to his seat.

He sipped his wine and his free hand sat on the table, with his nails tapping against it.

I took a sip of mine as well and let the sweet, effervescent taste wash over my tongue. "I wanted to thank you for saving me." I had not been able to get the attack out of my mind all day. Nor could I forget the softness he showed me after the attack.

"As long as you are a guest in my castle, I will strike down anything that tries to harm you." Fire burned in his ice-blue eyes, and my core melted.

He lifted his hand and snapped his fingers. Like every other time, the fae servants brought out dinner. They placed a plate in front of me, and a savory scent hit my nose. The most beautiful beef wellington sat on top of mashed potatoes with a side of roasted carrots.

"Would you like gravy, my lady?" The servant asked as he presented a silver gravy boat.

"Yes, please," I said with a smile.

He poured the gravy on top of the meat, and I watched as it pooled, and then dripped down the side. My mouth salivated, and I could not wait to devour it. Taking my fork and knife, I cut into the wellington, taking the medium rare meat into my mouth, which almost immediately melted. I could taste the savory umami of the mushroom duxelles as it hit my tongue.

Ezra leaned forward. He had not even touched his food. I sat down my fork and stared back at him. Swallowing hard, I leaned back into my seat.

"Why are you looking at me like that?"

"Do you like it?" He questioned, his focus flicked down to my plate before returning to my face.

"Yes, it is very good." I raised my eyebrow. "You have never asked that before. What did you do to it?"

He leaned back in his seat, and his shoulders relaxed. "I made it," he said in a soft tone.

"What?" My jaw dropped and my eyes widened.

"I prepared it," he said again, this time a little louder. "You told me to surprise you, so I cooked tonight's meal."

"This is absolutely delicious! I did not expect a king to know how to cook." I picked up my fork and knife and continued eating.

"My younger sister taught me." He finally picked up his fork and started to eat. "She wanted to be a chef, not a princess." He let out a soft chuckle, and he looked off in the distance. The sad expression on his face told me everything I needed to know. We stayed silent for a little while as we ate.

"I am sorry about your family," I finally broke the silence. "Gil told me what happened."

Ezra's gaze snapped toward me, and fire returned to his eyes. His lips pressed into a straight line. We stayed there for a moment, gazes locked before his face softened and returned to sadness. "Just another thing the curse has taken from me." He shrugged and continued eating.

"You never told me why the fae were cursed."

Ezra clenched his jaw and twirled the fork in between his fingers. "Long ago, a human girl crossed into Orilon and met my grandfather. She told my grandfather life across the portal was terrible and she never wanted to return. He provided her refuge within the castle and they fell in love. When her sister came looking for her, she begged my grandfather to keep her safe." He stabbed the fork into the dark wood of the table. "My grandfather lied to her, saying her sister died. That the wilds of Orilon claimed her. In a fit of rage, she cursed the fae to turn into horrible beasts. Turns out, she was no mere human, but a sorceress. Over the years, more and more fae turned into these creatures."

I could feel my heart break as he spoke. I thought the fae to all be horrid creatures, but the monsters I feared were created by a human. All along, it was the fae who wanted to keep a human safe.

"She added only one way to escape the curse. The fae king would bear a strange mark," he continued. "He would have five hundred years to find a human with the same mark and fall in love. My grandfather was the first to turn into the vox as soon as the curse was placed. He had no hope of finding the human with his mark. Even if he did, it wouldn't matter. He loved my grandmother more than anything in this universe."

His grandmother was human. The man who I feared, who hated humans, and ruled over the fae, was part human.

"My father never gained his mark. I had nearly given up before I found you. This was my final year to find someone with *my* mark."

He slowly unbuttoned his shirt and revealed an eight-point star birthmark under his collarbone.

It matched the one on my wrist perfectly.

"So, when you saw mine..." I said softly.

"Yes," he nodded. "I am so terribly sorry to pull you into this mess. You now understand time is truly of the essence."

"I understand." I took another bite and looked away.

"Let's talk about something lighter, shall we?" He gave me a soft smile that didn't reach his eyes. "How about some dessert?"

"Sounds lovely," I smiled back at him.

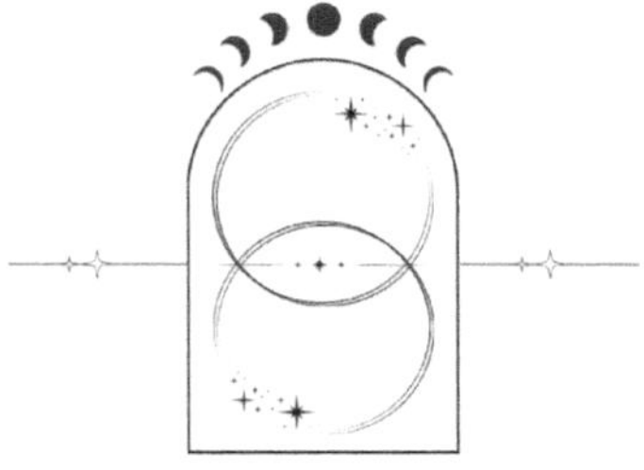

Twelve

I was so excited when Poppy told me Ezra planned to show me more of the gardens today. He wrapped his arm around me and held me close as we made our way through the main section, his shadows surrounded us to keep us safe from any plants that wished me to be their next meal. A door in the back of the garden led to yet another greenhouse. Rows of garden boxes with perfectly organized herbs filled the space. Around the perimeter were beds filled with pink roses.

"I thought this may be your favorite part of the gardens," Ezra said with a smile.

I stepped away from him and took a closer look at the garden box in front of us. It had some of the rarest herbs I had ever seen. Glenda would have absolutely freaked out if she saw them. I could already hear her now listing off all the elixirs she could make with these.

"This is wonderful," I said softly.

"What are you thinking about? Your eyes are looking elsewhere."

"Just thinking of my aunt. I miss her so much."

"I am sorry, sunshine. You will see her again soon. I promise you that."

I let out a sigh in response and turned away from his gaze. It was then I noticed the garden box filled with what looked to be vitella but was in multiple colors. My eyes went wide and a huge smile crossed my face. Back home, the vitella had green blooms. Here the blooms were blue, red, and purple. I walked over to the box to examine them more closely.

"Aren't they wonderful?" Ezra asked from behind me.

"I have never seen vitella in these colors. This is vitella, isn't it?"

"It is." Ezra walked over to my side. "Here in Orilon is where the vitella originated. Only the green variety made it across the portal and into the human realm. The others are not able to survive in the human world. I suppose they hate the mundane soil. Each color has slightly different properties. The green can help speed healing, but the red can elongate your life. The purple is actually a poisonous variety that steals the life from those who ingest it for the giver to take."

"That is fascinating!" I exclaimed.

"Any time you want to come here, please let Poppy know. I will happily escort you through the main garden to keep you safe."

"Thank you, Ezra."

"You're welcome, sunshine."

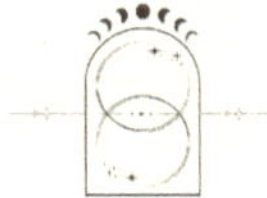

The next three days were filled with Ezra and I spending time with each other in the library and the gardens. Each evening, Ezra would prepare dinner for us to eat together. I hated to admit it, but the fae king was not so terrible to be around. Gods, if only I could tell Glenda and Jade of the man I met 'across the mountains'.

We sat after dinner, enjoying our lemon cream pie and talking about the books we read today in the library. Ezra also enjoyed the same books I did, which I found quite hilarious.

"Tomorrow I will not be able to join you in the gardens or the library. I have business to attend to." He took another bite of his pie.

"Business?" I tried to hide the disappointment on my face. After spending so much time with him, I truly enjoyed his company.

He let out a deep sigh. "Yes, unfortunately as king, I can't spend every day lounging around with you. Even if that is more enjoyable than what I need to get done."

I chuckled. "Oh? Did you just admit that you enjoy spending time with a human?"

"I would never admit such a thing," he said with a smirk.

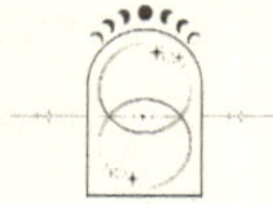

I spent all of the next day in the library, nestled in my reading nook. Staring out the window, I watched the rain hit the glass. Water droplets trailed down the glass, putting me in a relaxed state. The book I was reading could not hold my interest, I kept putting it down to watch more of the rain. The library had been very quiet, and I had not seen Gil all day. I wondered what he was up to today.

I really enjoyed speaking with Gil. He always had great book recommendations. They were always outside of my normal genre, but each of them ended up being amazing reads. I sat down the book I was reading and went to find him, hoping he would have a suggestion for me.

I wandered through the full library and was not able to find Gil. I looked over toward the door. Walking over to it, I peeked my head out and looked both ways, finding the hall empty. I decided to leave the library and explore. Wandering through the maze of hallways and staircases, I quickly found myself in a part of the castle I did not recognize.

I had gotten myself lost. I had no idea how to get back to the library. Most of the doors were shut and locked. Only one door had been opened and the room beyond it was empty.

I found a black wooden door with a golden doorknob at the end of a long hallway. The other doors had been natural wood. I twisted the handle, and beyond the door was a downward staircase made of dark stone. Closing the door behind me, I made my way down the stairs quietly. The sconces on the walls were covered in dust and cobwebs. Paintings were either crooked on the wall or had fallen completely. Stagnate must filled the air. At the bottom of the stairs, I found another maze of hallways.

I continued to walk down the halls, and the sound of my footsteps echoed. After a little while of traveling through the labyrinth of hallways, I realized I was lost.

My heart pounded in my chest. Panic was creeping in as I had no idea how I was going to get back to my room or the library from here. A familiar and terrifying screech sounded off from behind me. I turned and my heart dropped as I saw a vox. It was hunched over, claws dragging on the floor, with its blood-red eyes locked on me. I slowly took a step back, wanting as much distance between the two of us as possible.

It let out another scream, and its wings flared open as it sprinted toward me. I spun and took off running for my life. The monster made loud clicking noises as if it were communicating. Never had I heard those sounds come from the vox. More screeches and clicking filled the halls, but I was too afraid to look behind me. Tears ran down my face. This would be my end. No one had been in this section of the castle in years. This is where I would die, and no one would find my body. That is if the vox left a body to be found. Tears fell down my face and blurred my vision as I frantically searched for an escape.

I turned a corner and quickly regretted it. At the end of the hall sat a dead end, where a black suit of armor, which held a spear, faced me. I rushed to it and tried to yank away the spear, but it was stuck in place. Turning my head, I saw three vox now standing at the end of the hall. Baring their fangs, they progressed down the hall, slowly.

I was trapped.

I screamed and sobbed, still trying to free the spear. Shadows filled the space in between me and the vox, and Ezra emerged from them, his wings flared. This was the first time I saw them on full display. They were truly magnificent. The black of his wings were devoid of all light, causing the gold within them to shine. He flapped them hard and shadows rushed forward, forcing the vox to stagger back. The shadows enveloped them, and more of their screeches echoed off the walls. The shadows recoiled, and the vox fell to the floor. Their bodies shriveled, as if life was sucked out of them and their once red eyes were now a dull grey.

Ezra turned toward me, tucking his wings behind his back. Rage contorted his face. "I told you not to roam the castle!" His voice was filled with anger and boomed off the walls, causing me to cower. I finally looked into his eyes, and they were solid black. "*This* is why. You could have been killed!"

"I... I'm sorry," I whimpered.

Ezra grabbed me by the arm and yanked me toward him, squeezing so hard that I let out a yelp. "You would have been more than sorry if you had gotten hurt," he snarled. In a sudden motion, he lifted me and threw me over his shoulder. I did not fight him. The grasp he had lessened slightly, but he still held firm. I turned my head so I could look forward to see what Ezra was doing. He twisted the head of the suit of armor and the side wall slid open, revealing a secret passage.

I opened my mouth to speak, but as the first sound escaped my lips, Ezra cut me off. "Don't. I do not want to hear what you have to say." His voice was cold and distant.

We walked through the secret tunnel in silence. Tears still flowed down my face as we made our way. The torches on the wall illuminated as we reached them, and extinguished as we passed. After a while, Ezra pulled on one of the torches and the wall opened.

He sat me down and guided me into a small room with a desk, a library cart, and books. A shut door was on the far wall. The door to the secret tunnel shut behind us. Ezra looked down at me. The look of anger was gone, but the new expression was now much worse.

Disappointment.

"This," he pointed to the door at the far end of the room, "opens to the library. You will return to your room and Poppy will bring you dinner." He turned away and walked to the door, twisting the knob. The door did not budge. He pulled harder, his muscles flexed.

"Stop messing around. Let us out."

"The door is stuck," he said plainly as he stepped away from it.

"Then let's go back through the secret tunnel and find another exit!" All I wanted to do was to crawl into bed.

After what just happened, I wanted a safe quiet place to hide.

"It does not work that way," he sighed. "The door doesn't open from this side. Unfortunately, I used up a lot of my magic fighting the vox. My reserves are not as large as they used to be. Just another effect of the curse." He sat down on the floor and leaned his back against the wall. "We are stuck here until Gil comes back and finds us. This is his office, so he has to come here at some point."

"Some point?"

He nods. "Either until he finds us or my magic replenishes. Get comfortable, sunshine, we could be here for a while."

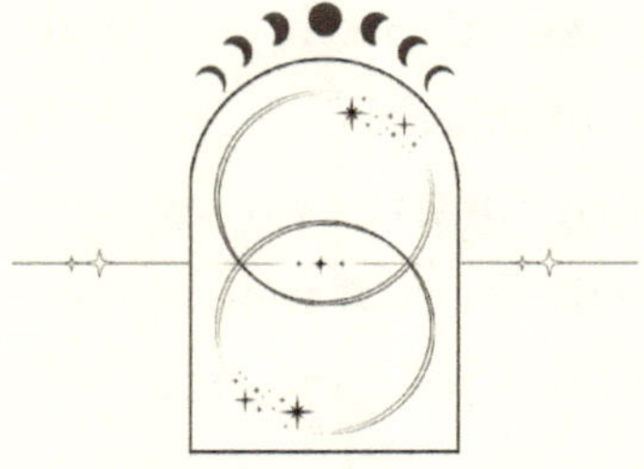

Thirteen

We sat in silence for an hour. Ezra grabbed a book off of Gil's desk and had been reading it for a while now. It was impossible to tell how much time had passed. I grabbed a book as well, but I could not focus on it. I was still shaken from the attack, and from the way Ezra reacted when he found me. I was thankful to him for saving me, but he showed me why he was the fae king. His power was beyond my comprehension. I will never forget the anger in his eyes.

Heat built in the room, and I felt sweat bead on my hairline and drip down my face. Ezra seemed totally unaffected by the heat, and I could not help but stare at him as he flipped through the pages of the book. After a while, he closed the book and sat it by his side. He didn't even look at me or say a word before removing his shirt, in one swift movement. Sweat glistened on his chest, and I blushed hard before looking away.

"Is that really necessary?" I looked back at him, trying not to stare at his muscles.

"It is hot." He finally looked toward me. "Your wandering gaze is not my problem." He sneered and then smirked. "You could remove your shirt and make it even." A deep chuckle escaped his throat, and he offered me a wink.

"You are such a pervert! I will absolutely *not* be doing that." I rolled my eyes, then focused my attention back to my book. Frustration built within me, as I hated I was attracted to him.

There was silence for a long moment before he answered. "Can you blame me? I am trapped with a beautiful woman."

"You think I am beautiful?" Heat filled my cheeks as I looked back up at him.

"I have told you many times. I am now ending this conversation." His gaze returned to his book. "I am still mad at you."

"I said I was sorry!" I huffed. Sitting my book in my lap, I crossed my arms.

"Amara." His tone lowered and softened, causing my heart to skip a beat. "If you had gotten hurt..." His voice trailed off as he closed the book and sat it down again. Pushing off the wall, he slowly crawled to me. His ice-blue eyes never looked away from mine. When his face was just a few inches from mine, he stopped. His two braids hung in the space between us. "I don't know what I would have done."

My body tensed as he got closer. Every part of me screamed for me to close the gap between us. I took in a deep breath of the electrified air and bit my bottom lip, trying to force those thoughts away. "Because if I died, we couldn't break the curse?"

"Well, yes." He smirked. "Though there are other reasons."

"Other reasons?" My voice shook as I spoke. My mind raced at all the possibilities. I thought his kindness all had to do with him needing me to break the curse. Could he have gained feelings beyond that?

He leaned in just a little more, and my heart pounded harder. I swore my chest was about to explode. Just before our lips touched, he quickly pulled back. In a blink, he was back against the wall, reading his book again.

The door swung open, and Gil looked down at us and let out a laugh. I looked up at him in shock. Ezra didn't even look up from the book. "There you two are! We have been looking for you everywhere."

Quickly, I jumped up. Ezra, still shirtless, slowly stood with an air of grace, flicked his hair back behind his shoulder, and walked out. As he passed Gil, he stopped and looked down at him. "Will you take Amara to her room? I must return to my duties."

"Yes, Your Majesty," he said with a nod.

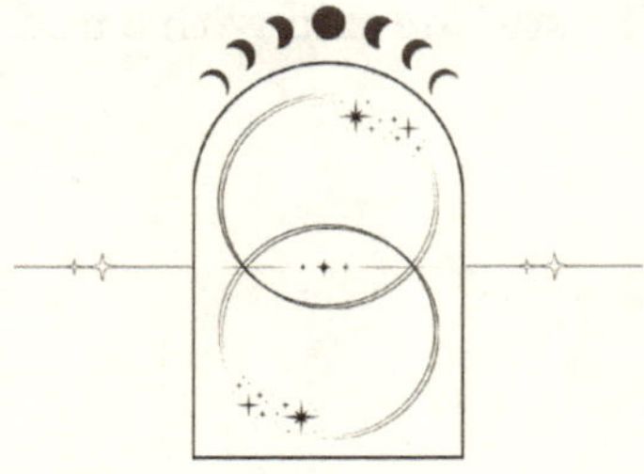

Fourteen

After being returned to my room, Poppy brought up a dinner of roasted lamb. Once she put my meal on the table and offered me a greeting, she left. I sat at the table by the window overlooking the forest, pushing around the peas that sat on my plate.

I found myself totally overwhelmed by what happened. Why had I been so drawn to leave the library? I knew better than to do that. Normally, I was so cautious. How did Ezra find me in that final moment? How did the fates weave this tale, and how would they continue to?

My body heated at the thought of Ezra, shirtless. I hated I loved the way he looked. When he was so close,

I craved his touch and wished he had closed the gap between our lips.

What I hated even more was Gil interrupting us.

Thoughts continued to race through my mind. Did Ezra truly feel that way? Did he have feelings for me, or was it just the heat of the moment fueled by the romance he was reading?

My dinner had gone cold while I was busy running through all the thoughts trapped in my head. I pushed it away, folded my arms down on the desk, laid my head down, and stared out at the soft purple glow in the distance. A firm knock pulled me out of my daydream, and I sat straight up.

"Who is it?" I called out.

"It is I." His deep, smooth voice was like music to my ears.

I jumped from my seat, calling for him to come in. The door swung open, and Ezra stepped in. He looked down at me, took a deep breath, and shut the door behind him. We stayed locked in each other's gazes for a silent moment.

My heart pounded in my chest, and I twiddled with my thumbs as I anxiously awaited for him to speak.

"I apologize for how I reacted earlier. I was so angry with you. You disobeyed the rules and endangered yourself." He took a step closer to me. "I should not have spoken to you the way I did. I understand you think the rules are to keep you trapped. I promise on the heart of my kingdom they are in place to keep you safe." He spoke in a firm, yet gentle tone.

"I am sorry for wandering off. It will never happen again," I whimpered, looking down and away from him.

"Very good. Good night, Amara."

My head snapped up. "Wait!"

Ezra had been reaching for the door, but quickly turned toward me, hope gleaming in his eyes. "Yes?"

"You never answered my question."

"What question?" A smirk formed on his lips.

"What were the other reasons?"

Ezra closed the gap between us. My heart pounded and heat rose to my cheeks as he gently lifted my chin, his thumb gently brushing my bottom lip. "If something had happened to you," desire burned in his eyes, "I couldn't do this." He softly pressed his lips to mine. His arm wrapped around my waist to hold me close, and his spicy citrus scent filled my nose.

I was glad he did because, without his support, I would have fallen to the floor when my knees buckled as I got on my tippy toes to press into the kiss.

After a moment, he pulled his lips away. A hollowness took over the space where the heat of his touch had been.

"Sunshine, your kisses taste like sweet nectar from the gods. Will you allow me another taste?"

I slammed my lips back into his as my response. The passion grew between us as I wrapped my arms around his neck as we kissed. His tongue slipped into my mouth and danced with mine as he held me closer. Heat flooded me, and I released a curse as he released me and pulled away. His shadows flared around him.

"Good night, sunshine. I will see you tomorrow." With that final word, he stepped back and vanished into his shadows.

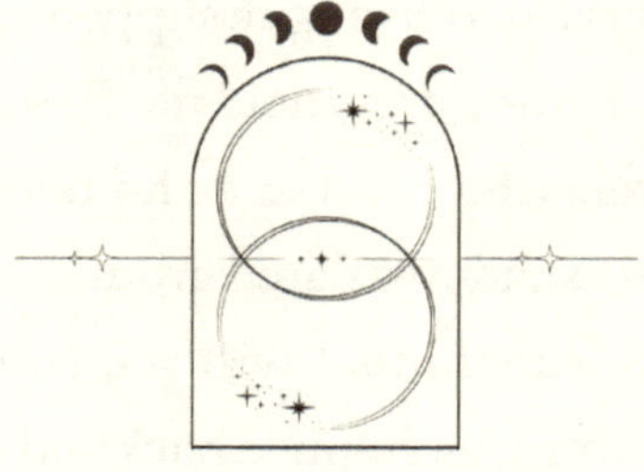

Fifteen

"Amara." Poppy's voice jolted me awake. I felt her hand on my shoulder, gently shaking me.

"I'm up," I yawned. "I'm up." I sat up and stretched my arms above my head. Looking out the window, I saw the moon still hung in the sky among a sea of stars. I looked over to Poppy, confused. "What time is it?"

"Early. Get up. I have to get you ready. The king requests your immediate company!"

My eyes widened in shock. "Why now? Can't it wait a few hours until dawn?"

"No! Now, get up!" She let out a huff, as did I.

I got out of bed and allowed Poppy to get me ready. She styled my blonde bob into soft curls and placed me in a light purple knee-length dress. Once I was ready, we quickly made our way to the library. Ezra was already waiting.

"Good morning, Amara," he said with a smile. His voice was way too chipper for this hour. "Since you are so set on exploring, you and I will be taking a little trip today. We must make haste, as we are already late. Come along." Ezra quickly turned on his heels and walked away. Waving goodbye to Poppy, I followed him.

"Are you going to tell me where we are going?" I quickened my pace to keep up with his stride.

"No," he chuckled. Turning toward the wall, he twisted the sconce and the wall slipped open to reveal a hidden path. He ushered me into the secret passage, following close behind. Once we were both in, he closed the entrance. For a while, we walked side by side in a hall with no windows. It took me a while to realize this was not a man-made hallway, but a tunnel carved out of solid stone. I begged him for any information on where we were going, but he refused to give in.

Finally, sunlight could be seen in the distance. As my eyes adjusted to the warm glow, it revealed we now stood on a mountainside cliff. The sun had just risen over the peaks. On the ground sat a red blanket with a basket sitting atop it.

"I thought you would enjoy some fresh air," he said with a smile as warm as the sun.

I walked closer to the edge of the cliff, and my jaw dropped as I took in the view. Nestled in a small gap below ran a creek. White stags with rainbow iridescent antlers drank. I had never seen such a beautiful creature in my entire life. I turned back to Ezra, who was standing next to the basket.

"I baked fruit and cheese danishes. I did not know what kind of fruit you liked, so I made a few different kinds." He sat down next to the basket and laid out its contents.

I sat next to him, looking over the options, and decided on the lemon. I took a bite, and the bright flavor filled my mouth. The pastry was so flakey and light, and the sugar crystals that were baked on top gave it a nice crunch.

"This is divine," I said as I took another bite. "Thank you!"

"You are so welcome." He grabbed an apple danish and took a bite. Once he swallowed, he spoke again. "Since we are now so close to the wedding, I wanted to check on you. How are you feeling?"

I took another bite, thinking about that for a moment. "Honestly, I am alright. I am still very worried about my aunt. She must be worried sick about me, at this point she may presume me to be dead."

"I took care of that," he said plainly.

"What do you mean?" I lowered my pastry.

"I visited her the day I took you and glamoured her memories. She thinks you are delivering herbs to the capital."

"How did you know who she was to do that?" I raised my eyebrow. A pit grew in my stomach.

"I followed your scent."

"My scent? What do I smell like?"

"Honey and lavender," he said without a single thought. "A scent that is sweet and calming. A scent of love and kindness. A scent of sunshine and home."

Heat rose to my cheeks. I stared into Ezra's eyes, truly mesmerized, and too stunned to speak. He offered me a smile that did not reach those gorgeous ice-blue eyes.

"Amara?" He questioned softly, snapping me out of my own head.

"How do you feel about the wedding? Are you excited to send me back to the human realm?"

This was it. This was my moment to get the answers I needed. Did he truly care for me, or was I just a new shiny toy to pass his time?

He turned his head to look over the cliff and released a deep, slow breath. "I can't wait to not have a little human sneaking around my castle and taking up my time."

My heart shattered.

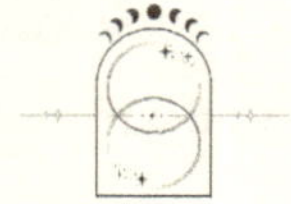

That afternoon, I found myself back in the library. I chose the book Ezra was reading while we were trapped in the office, squirming in my seat as the romance heated up. I heard light footsteps from behind one of the shelves.

"Hello?"

"It's me!" I heard Poppy's cheerful voice.

I shut the book and sat it on my lap. "I am back in the reading nook!" I called out to her.

Her footsteps quickened, and shortly she was by my side and sitting next to me.

"Did you enjoy your breakfast while you watched the sunrise?" She gently bumped me with her shoulder.

"It was lovely. I was happy to get some fresh air." I shrugged. My heart still ached from the rejection I received from Ezra. Part of me hoped he truly cared for me. What a silly little human I was to think that.

"And you agreed to stay with us, right?" Her voice rose in pitch, and she quickly clapped her hands.

My gaze snapped to her and raised my eyebrow. "What did you say?"

"Didn't Ezra ask for you to stay with us after the wedding?" Her excited expression dropped, and concern took over.

"No, he said he could not wait for me to return to the human realm."

Anger took over Poppy's face. "He is such a coward!" She jumped up, grabbed my wrist, and pulled me to follow her. Yanked from my seat, I stumbled before I caught up to her pace.

"Where are we going?"

"To speak with the king!"

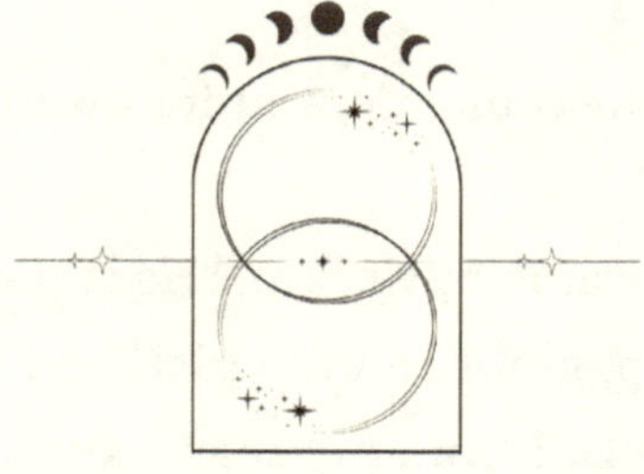

Sixteen

Poppy dragged me through the halls, pulling me into sections of the castle I had never seen. My heart pounded in my chest. I worried about what lurked within the shadows, but then I remembered shadows were his domain.

"Poppy! Stop it! I am not allowed to be in this part of the castle."

She ignored my pleas and continued charging ahead, pulling me behind her. Finally, she released my wrist as she stopped in front of a large black wooden door with golden accents. Poppy yanked the door open and barged in.

Ezra stood in the center of the room in front of his bed with a towel wrapped around his waist. His damp hair fell loose over his shoulders. A look of terror crossed his face. "Excuse me, ladies?"

"Why did you not ask her to stay?" Poppy blurted out, stomping her feet and crossing her arms.

Embarrassment took over Ezra's face. "Poppy," he sighed, "it is complicated. She has a family to return to."

"You didn't even ask her! She may have said yes!" She grabbed a vase that was on a nearby table and threw it at him. He easily stepped away from it, causing it to shatter against the wall behind him.

"Enough!" His voice boomed. "Poppy, leave us."

"Gladly!" She turned and stormed off. Winking at me as she left. The door slammed behind me, causing me to flinch.

Ezra turned toward me, a softness in his eyes. "I apologize for her behavior."

"Were you going to ask me to stay after the wedding?" My voice quivered as I spoke.

"Never mind that." He threw his hands in the air and turned away.

"No! Do not try to change the subject. Answer me!" I demanded.

He turned back toward me, dropping his shoulders in defeat. "Yes, but I understand you would not want to stay here with me."

I stared at him for some time, taking in a deep breath as I collected my thoughts. "I could not leave my aunt behind permanently. Would I be able to visit her? And my best friend?"

His eyes lit up, and a smile crossed his face. "With an escort, yes. As my wife, you would be Queen of Orilon. It would be dangerous for you to travel alone."

"How often?" I raised my eyebrow, stepping closer to him.

"As often as you wish. You are not a prisoner, Amara. You never were." He inhaled sharply, tightening his jaw. Silence hung in the air for a moment. "Will you stay with me? Please, be my true wife. Not just to break the curse, but until the world ends and we are nothing but stardust."

I smirked. "I shall think about it."

"Oh, sunshine, it would be an honor." He smirked back at me.

"Oh, I am sure it would be."

"Just as it is an honor for you to gaze upon me in a towel. Do not think I have not noticed your staring."

Heat rushed to my cheeks. "We are speaking! Where do you want me to look? The ground?"

He closed the gap between us and wrapped his arms around my waist, pressing my body to his. I felt something firm press into my stomach that caused my core to ache with need. "Oh, sunshine, you weren't looking at my face. Ask nicely, and I will show you what you want to see," he teased.

"I... I do not know what you are talking about," I stumbled over my words. I felt as if I could melt in his arms.

A devilish grin spread across his face. "Let me show you." His shadows slivered up from behind me and wrapped around my body. Ezra released me and stepped back. His shadows pulled me to the bed, forced me to sit on the edge, and then held my face, making me look forward.

"Ezra," I breathed.

He dropped his towel, revealing his full length to me. Air caught in my throat from the sight of it. Good gods, I had never seen anything so magnificent.

"If you ask nicely, I will allow you to touch it." His shadows wrapped around me tighter and rubbed against my thighs and breasts.

A soft moan escaped my lips. "Who said I wanted to?" What a lie. I wanted nothing more than for him to tear off my clothes and take me. I could not look away from his fist that slowly pumped his fully erect cock.

Ezra leaned down so we met eye to eye. "I can see it in your eyes, sunshine." He bit his bottom lip, and fire burned in those ice-blue eyes. At this close proximity, his scent drove me wild, nearly distracting me as the shadows slithered up my skirt and teased the fabric between my legs.

I squirmed as shadows played against my most sensitive parts. "Ezra," I moaned.

He cut me off before I could say anything. "The only thing that should come out of your pretty little mouth is 'yes, sir' and moans. Do you understand?"

"Yes, sir." My body tensed as I spoke the words and let Ezra command me.

"Good girl. Now spread your legs and let my shadows explore that beautiful body of yours." His tongue slowly dragged over his top lip as he straightened his back and continued to fist himself, quickening the pace.

I obliged, spreading my legs and leaning back. The shadows pulled off my clothes, exposing me to the King of Orilon. The man I once hated. The man I once feared... before I knew his soul.

My core melted as his shadows wrapped around my bare breasts, squeezing them, and flicking my nipples. Another of his shadow tendrils found its way back between my thighs and gently lapped at my delicate skin. It then slowly slipped inside me, causing me to arch my back.

"Please," I begged.

The shadow pumped faster inside of me. Ezra arched a brow, and the tendril pulled out of my aching pussy. "I didn't remember telling you that was one of the things you could say." The shadow whipped against my clit, causing me to release a yelp. Pressure and heat built within my core as the tendril slapped against me once again. "Please what?" His voice was deep and sensual. It alone could cause me to come undone.

"I need more," I pleaded.

"I will tell you what you need. Now not another word."

"Yes, sir." I bit my bottom lip, as I submitted to the king.

The shadow forced its way back inside me, opening me up. The ones around my breasts flicked harder. My attention could not pull away from Ezra's cock. The sight of him was everything. I found myself so close to the edge as pleasure built inside me.

"Don't you dare cum until I tell you to," he snarled.

"Yes, sir." I held it in, allowing the ecstasy of it to take over my body. I couldn't allow myself release. Not until he gave me permission, which only added to the thrill.

"You are such a good girl for me. Use your words. Tell me what you want."

"I need your cock inside me. I need to cum. Please," I moaned. My body was so close to exploding. The shadows recoiled, leaving me feeling empty.

"Get on your knees. Open your mouth," he demanded.

Again, I obliged, quickly getting onto the floor. My knees rested on the black and gold rug as I stuck out my tongue for him. He stepped closer and smirked down at me as he rested his tip on my tongue. I slowly licked and teased it. My hand gently massaged his balls as I dragged my tongue from base to tip.

Ezra let out a groan, ran his fingers through my hair, and gripped it to hold me in place. Taking his tip into my mouth, I gently sucked, swirling my tongue against his sensitive head. Looking up at him, I carefully watched his expression. Ezra tilted his head back in pleasure as he bucked into my mouth.

His shadows found their way in between my legs once again and quickly thrust into my dripping slit. I moaned against him as I took him deeper down my throat.

In opposite rhythms, Ezra's cock and shadow thrust in and out of me, and I quickly found myself at the edge of pleasure once again. His pace quickened as he hit the back of my throat, and my saliva dripped down his balls.

He pushed forward, holding himself deep down my throat, and my nose pressed against his bare skin. I could barely hold in my pleasure. It would not be much longer before I lost control and disobeyed him.

"Cum for me, sunshine," he groaned.

My eyes rolled back in my head as, for the first time in my life, I experienced true bliss. I let out a moan around him, causing him to twitch in the back of my throat. My entire body quivered, and I craved more of him. I bobbed my mouth from base to tip as our eyes stayed locked on each other.

His shadow left me once again, leaving a puddle dripping out of me. He then slowly pulled himself from my mouth, reached down, and pulled me to my feet. Spinning me around, he grabbed me by my hair and pushed me down on the bed, my legs hanging off.

"You thought my shadow felt good?" He leaned down and whispered in my ear. "Just wait until you feel the real thing." In a swift motion, Ezra plunged his cock into me. The shadows were nothing compared to the real thing. He showed me no mercy as he made me his. He pulled on my hair, causing my back to arch.

I gripped the sheets and screamed in pleasure, begging him not to stop.

He was right. This was nothing like I had ever felt. The immense pleasure sent me over the edge once again, without permission. I clenched around him as I found my release.

Ezra let out a growl. "Fuck, you're going to pay for that," he groaned, as he pulled my hair tighter. "Tell me what you just did."

"I came," I squealed.

"For who?" He thrust in hard.

"You!"

"Only for me?" He pulled out almost all the way.

"Only for you!"

He pounded into me harder. I ached as he thrusted, and I screamed his name.

"That's right, Amara. You are mine." Heat filled me as he spilled into me. He did not slow his pace but instead pushed his release deeper. I moaned and begged for him not to stop. He continued to fuck me until I found my release once again.

Only then did he finally pull out of me and spin me around. A hunger still filled his eyes as I looked up at him, breathless.

"Are you ready for round two?" A predatory grin crossed his face.

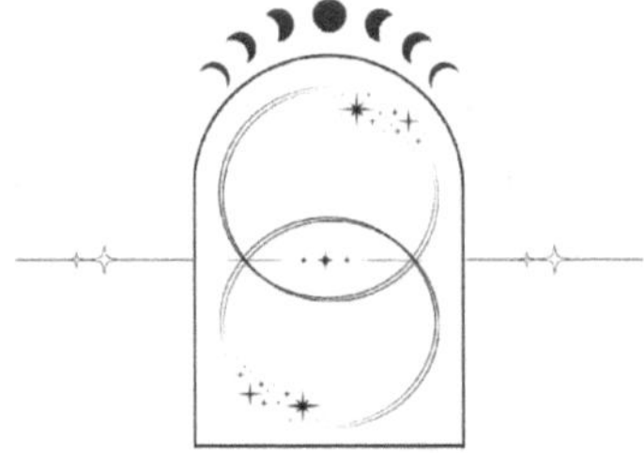

Seventeen

The soft sound of birdsong awoke me from the best sleep I had ever had. Sitting up, I gave a small yawn, stretching out in front of me. I spent the entire night in Ezra's bed, though we did not fall asleep until the moon was past its peak. Last night was more perfect than I could ever imagine. Never did I expect my first time to be like that. Before I met Ezra, I did not think there would be a first time for me.

I was always so content being alone. Living my life as the town herbalist, and taking one of my friends' children under my wing to continue the craft. Once my eyes locked on Ezra, everything changed, even if I hated to admit it. He was everything in a man I had been looking for.

Jade would be so happy I found a man across the mountains who brought me this much joy and pleasure.

I looked over and saw the glass door to the balcony open. The sun was shining directly on Ezra, just another sign from the heavens that he and I were meant as one. His dark black robe was wrapped around him as he sipped his mug of coffee.

Slipping out of bed, still nude, I slipped on the ivory silk robe that had been laid out for me and tied it shut. The plush rug was so soft against my bare feet as I exited the room and joined Ezra on the balcony. Nipping at my nose, the cool morning air blew against my face.

"Good morning, sunshine," Ezra said before I could speak. "Would you like a cup of coffee?"

"Good morning. Yes, please! That sounds delightful." Sitting in the chair across the table from him, I watched as he poured my cup. A small tray sat on the glass table with cream and cubes of sugar. Once he handed me my mug, I added more sugar and cream than was good for one person.

"I am glad I asked for it," Ezra chuckled. "I drink my coffee black."

"That is a terrible way to live!" I smiled as I took my sip. The hot sweetness rushed down my throat and warmed my core.

"I quite enjoy the strong and bitter taste."

Sitting back in my seat, I pressed my mug against my cheek, and shut my eyes.

"You look truly beautiful," Ezra said softly.

"Thank you." I smiled. Even though the events that led me to be here with him were not ideal, I could not be happier with the way everything was turning out.

There was another moment of silence before Ezra spoke again. "Was it ok? Did I hurt you?"

My eyes jolted open, and I turned toward him. "It was amazing!"

"Good, good." His gaze fell to his mug. "I did not want to disappoint."

"Disappoint?"

"I am a disappointment to my entire kingdom. I would not be surprised if I was a disappointment to you, too."

I leaned over and placed my hand atop his that held the handle of his mug. His gaze lifted to meet mine. "You are not a disappointment. You will save your kingdom. I promise you that."

"Thank you, Amara," he choked on his words. Ezra cleared his throat and straightened his back. "I will be away for a few days. Final preparations need to be made for the wedding. The seamstress is coming to meet with you today to design your dress. Have her create whatever your heart desires. Poppy will take you to meet with her."

"How are you going to give me the best night of my life and then leave me?"

"It will just make you crave me more." Ezra stood and walked over to me, leaning down and kissing my forehead gently. "I will be back soon. I will make up for all the pleasure lost as soon as I return."

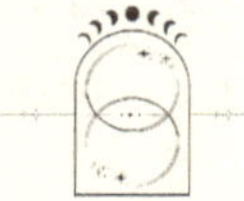

That afternoon, Poppy took me into a new section of the castle. She led me into a room with a small circular stage in the center of the room. The stage was about one foot high and solid black stone. Next to it, there were racks and racks of different fabrics, corsets, and embellishments. A large window was on the far wall, filling the room with natural light.

"Good afternoon." A short woman with long and straight dark hair approached me. She wore a beautiful purple dress. Around her waist was a belt that dangled all sorts of tools of a seamstress. Her teal eyes were filled with joy as she took my hand. "What a joyous time!"

"Yes, I am very excited! I have never had a custom dress made!" I gleamed as the seamstress helped me step onto the stage.

Poppy walked over to the racks and looked at the different lace fabrics. "Wow, I don't know how you are going to pick!"

"Yes, you're getting married to the king. You must look your best. What kind of idea of a dress are you looking for?"

"I would love a big, beautiful ballroom-style dress. I want to look and feel like a princess!" To be honest, I had never thought about the type of dress I would wear, since I never believed this was going to happen to me. But now it was happening, I wanted to go all out for the big day. I had seen many weddings back home, and the ballroom-style dresses were always my favorite.

The seamstress slowly circled me, her eyes scanning me. "That could work. But, remember dear. You are no princess. You will be a queen. Let me help you down so you can change into a slip, and we can get to work."

She assisted me down and took me over to a changing screen. Slipping out of my olive-green dress, I put on the ivory slip. I got back onto the stage and the seamstress pulled out different corsets and fabrics. Before I finalized, we went through twelve corsets and way too many lace patterns. I decided on a tulle with flowers embroidered throughout it.

Poppy gave her opinions on everything, she wanted me to have exactly what I wanted. The seamstress was so kind and helpful. She really helped me envision the dress, and I could not wait to see the final product.

"I have never met the king. What is he like?" The seamstress asked as she sketched out the final design.

"He is very kind." I offered her a small grin.

"That is good to hear!" She smiled and continued her sketches.

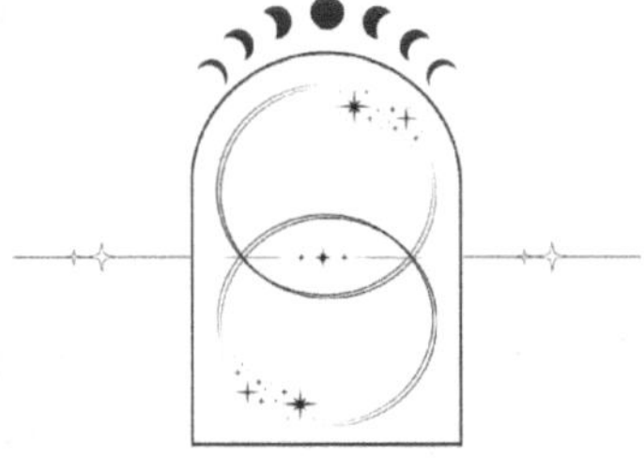

Eighteen

Days passed quickly as Poppy and I were busy finalizing things for the wedding. Every day was filled with meetings with the seamstress for fittings, picking floral arrangements, selecting a cake, and finalizing a dinner menu. I was surprised to hear this would be a large event. With very little fae left, I expected it just to be the priestess, Ezra, and myself.

Ezra told me the other realms turned their backs on Orilon when he first showed me the library. Now, with the wedding, they would all show up. Was it in support, or to see if Orilon was for the taking if the last king fell victim to the curse?

I was very interested in learning about the other fae realms. My whole life I had been told there was only one portal, but now I knew there were five more were hidden throughout Elswyth. Poppy did not know much about the other realms, but Gil had several books on the subject and was happy to hand them over.

Aeros sounded very interesting. It was a group of floating islands, high in the sky. Even though the fae of this realm were winged, little was known about the world below the islands. Legend claimed that the floating islands were once a part of the land below, but when calamity hit, the King of Aeros raised the capital city and surrounding lands to save them from disaster.

I found myself daydreaming about the realms as the seamstress finalized the dress. Only a few more tiny alterations to the straps needed to be made.

"I cannot believe how gorgeous this dress is!" Poppy squealed in delight.

My gaze snapped over to the mirror. She was right. The dress was perfect. The bodice had a sweetheart neckline and beautiful beading, making it sparkle. The bottom of the dress was a full skirt with beautiful floral lace. My eyes teared up from happiness. This was everything I imagined and more.

"You made this so quickly!" I looked over at the seamstress and smiled.

"I am the best seamstress of all the realms. This is what I do," she said nonchalantly as she organized her pins.

"I really do love it!" I did a little twirl, watching myself in the mirror.

"Thank you!" Her gaze raised to meet mine. "Are you nervous about marrying the king? Was this an arranged marriage? You seem like such an odd pair."

"It is a complicated situation..." My voice trailed off.

"Oh?" she pried as she knelt to pin the hem just a little higher.

"Well... the marriage was not exactly my first choice, but I am glad to have met him. I can't wait to see what unfolds." I gave Poppy a nervous glance. She sat just a few feet from the small stage on a stool, her eyes locked on the seamstress.

"You seem a bit apprehensive." The seamstress looked up at me with an inquisitive look. She stood and walked over to a small cart, and looked through a tiny box she brought with her.

It felt odd she was asking so many questions. I knew a lot of nosey women in my life. Growing up in a small village, I was way too familiar with women collecting all sorts of gossip.

"I was at first, but not so much anymore."

"How interesting." The seamstress walked back over to me and continued to work on my dress.

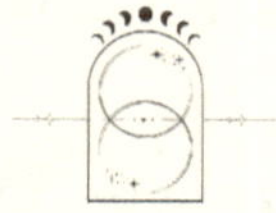

After the fitting wrapped up, I finally was able to get a moment of relaxation. Once again, I found myself in the library, curled up in my nook with a romance novel, shutting out the world around me. Just as I was fully enthralled by the book, shadows filled my peripheral vision.

"Did you miss me?" I heard his deep, velvet voice purr in my ear. A shiver sent down my spine as his shadows found their way under my dress once again.

As I closed the book, I quickly sat up. Ezra stood a few feet away, leaning against a bookshelf with his arms crossed and a predatory grin on his face.

Gods, how I missed those angular features. The moon on his third eye looked darker than it ever had as if it was the void itself. The shadows found their way under the thin fabric that was my only protection from them and teased the small bundle of nerves.

"Ezra, stop that! What if someone comes in here?" I let out a moan as the shadow slowly pushed its way inside me. Gods, it felt amazing, but it only made me crave the feeling of his cock.

Ezra walked over, stopping right before me. "Then they will see their king pleasuring his queen. I made you a promise before I left, and I plan to keep it." A low growl escaped his lips. The shadow's pace quickened, and my wetness grew. "Get on your knees."

I quickly did as I was told. Ezra released himself from his pants and gave it two strokes. A small bead of liquid pooled at the tip. Without hesitation, I slowly dragged my tongue against it to lick it away.

"Such an eager one you are," he purred.

"I won't lie. I missed your cock."

He knelt before me so that our eyes met. "And I missed that pretty little cunt of yours. Will you give me the honor of getting on your hands and knees, lifting your dress, and show me how you get fucked by my shadow?"

I spun around and did as I was told. I lifted my dress, and his hands gently removed my panties, leaving them around my knees. The shadow pounded into me harder. I let out a squeal as I found my pleasure.

"Oh, you are such a bad girl. You didn't ask permission." His shadow slowly pulled out of me.

"No, please don't stop!" I begged.

"Don't stop, what?" He spoke in a playful tone.

"Don't stop fucking me, please!"

It was silent for just a moment, then he thrust himself deep into me. His hands tightly gripped my hips, pulling me back onto his cock. My eyes rolled into the back of my head as I fully came undone around him. Gods, I loved how he made me feel.

Releasing my hips, one of his hands found its way in between my shoulder blades, pushing me down to the floor, pinning me in place as he fucked me. I screamed his name, begging for him never to stop.

He let out a groan as he pressed in firmly and held it. His cock twitched as he released himself inside me. I throbbed against him, craving all of him.

"I never expected to find such pleasure in my human queen," he groaned as he pulled out of me. In a blink, he was in front of me, sitting in the reading nook, his cock still erect. He slowly raised his hand, palm up, and called to me with two fingers. I crawled to him, kneeling in between his legs.

Without a word, I slowly dragged my tongue from base to tip. My gaze locked on his ice-blue eyes. He let out a groan and tilted his head back as I swirled around the tip. Ezra's hand found its way to my hair and laced his fingers through my golden curls, keeping me in place.

I wrapped my lips around his head and gently sucked as my hand lifted and stroked his length.

"Oh, fuck," he groaned, as he pushed my head down and forced me to take more of him into my mouth. He continued to push until I felt him hit the back of my throat, causing me to gag. He then pulled me back up by my hair, until my lips sat at the tip before forcing me down again. "Play with your pretty cunt while I fuck your throat," he demanded.

I found myself lifting my skirt and sliding my hand in between my thighs as I gagged and drooled on him. My fingers delicately teased the soaked entrance. Drool dripped down Ezra's balls as he continued to pound my throat.

Slipping my fingers inside, I quickly forced them in and out of me. Gods, I craved his cock inside my pussy once again. I knew I would never experience such pleasure by my own hand. Ezra held my head down and he released in the back of my throat. He did not pull away until I swallowed every last drop.

"Ezra," I moaned as I looked up at him.

"Amara, you are so perfect. I am so glad you have come into my life. Here, let me help you up." He put himself away and assisted me up off the floor. "Let's get you cleaned up, and then have a nice dinner on the balcony. How does that sound?"

"Amazing," I said with a smile.

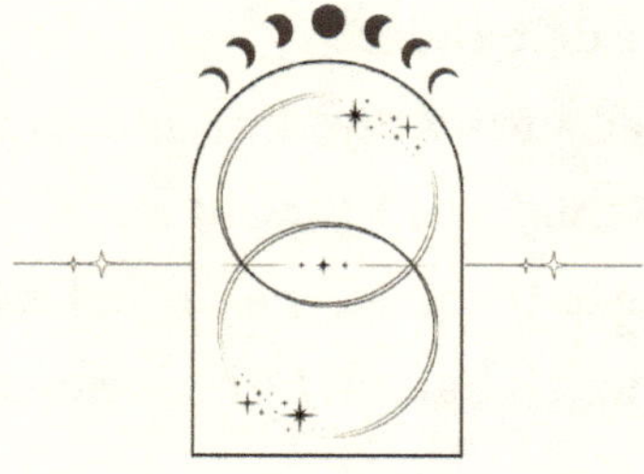

Nineteen

The day of the wedding came faster than I expected. I did not get a single moment of sleep the night before. It seemed so wrong to be wed without my aunt and Jade by my side. I was not ready for my new home to be filled with fae I did not know.

Before the guests arrived, I stayed in my room, hiding away. I accidentally ran into one of the first to arrive in the library yesterday morning. He was a tall, slender, older man, with cruelty in his eyes. I quickly ran away from him before he could speak.

Poppy told me he was the new King of Irolyth, just crowned a year ago. He had accused his brother of treason and had the entire royal family executed. The

Princess had gone missing during the siege on the castle. Still to this day, she has not been found.

Poppy said it had been a very messy affair, and she was worried for one of her sisters who had moved there decades ago to live in The Glade, a religious sanctuary. She had not heard from her in years.

The next morning, Poppy had awoken me very early and took me to the suite where I was to prepare for the wedding. So many people filled the halls, and all eyes were on me as we passed them. They never spoke a word to me, nor I to them. I could not help but wonder why they were all in the halls, instead of in their rooms or the dining hall for breakfast.

Anxiety crept in. My skin crawled, and I vigorously scratched at my arms. This was all becoming too real, too fast.

Poppy quickly spun to me and swatted at my hand. Quickly, she pulled us into an empty room and shut the door behind us. "Stop that! Do not dare damage that beautiful skin of yours on your big day! Most of these fae are from other kingdoms. You will not see them after today. Take a deep breath. Imagine they are all in their underwear!"

"Their underwear?!"

"Nudity is the greatest equalizer." She placed her hand on the door handle. "Now take a deep breath, follow me, and remember this will all be over soon and you can spend the rest of your days in marital bliss." She stared at me for a long while as I took in deep breaths to calm myself.

Once I was calm, she opened the door and exited the room. I followed behind her. This time, I ignored all of the strange faces that stared at me.

"We are almost there," she said as she continued to guide me, her auburn hair flowing. We entered the suite, and it was beautiful. Two white couches sat on either side of a glass coffee table. On the table were bright color flower arrangements. Golden sconces were on the walls and provided the windowless room with light. My dress was hung on a hook on the wall. I still could not believe how perfect it was. Crystals had been added to the skirt to cause it to sparkle. Two other girls who looked nearly identical to Poppy jumped from their seats.

"Amara, these are my sisters. Lily and Rose." She gestured to each of them as she introduced them. "The three of us will be getting you ready for your big day."

"I meant to ask you about that. I did not know you had any sisters."

"There are seven of us in total," Lily said with the same sense of joy her sister had.

"Daisy, Violet, and Iris could not make it. They are busy in their realms," Rose said, a bit more sass in her voice. "No one has heard from Cassia in about a year. We want to go check on her, but the gates to Irolyth have all closed."

"Gates? I thought each realm only had one gate?" I asked.

"Elswyth only has one gate to each realm. Within the fae realms, there are multiple gates to get to where we need to go," Lily answered.

"Never mind all that. Today is Amara's special day. Rose, please get started on our blushing bride's make-up!" Poppy snapped.

"Just because you think you're the oldest, it doesn't mean you get to be bossy," Rose retorted.

"But I am the oldest!" Poppy responded.

"By three minutes," Lily giggled.

"Come with me. I will make you look flawless," Rose said as she guided me over to a seat, shaking her head at her sisters. All kinds of makeup was laid out on the table in front of me. "This is what I am best at. Just let me work my magic, and you will be even more stunning than you already are!"

I believed her. While Lily and Poppy were beautiful, Rose was flawless.

While Rose worked on my makeup, Lily came and did my hair into loose curls. She wove in a flower crown with delicate pink and white flowers. When the two of them were done, I looked absolutely divine. Once ready the three of them helped me into my dress. When I finally looked at myself in the mirror, My breath was stolen away. Never had I seen myself so beautiful.

"Amara," the three of them gasped in unison. "You are so beautiful."

I couldn't help but start to tear up at the view of myself in the mirror.

"No! None of that!" Rose rushed to me and blotted my eyes. "You will ruin your makeup!" She pulled away the handkerchief and the golden dust that was on my eyes now stained it. She sighed, "come with me." She took me back to the makeup and touched up what had been smudged.

"Why are you crying?" Lily questioned.

"I just wish my aunt and best friend were here. This feels so wrong without them!"

"I am so sorry," they all cooed in unison.

"You will see them again soon," Poppy promised, putting her hand on my shoulder in comfort. I was thankful to have Poppy here with me. She had become such a good friend, but my heart still ached for my family in Pendril.

As Rose put on the finishing touches, a servant came into the suite. "The king is ready."

Lily and Rose both hugged me. "It was so lovely to meet you. I hope to see you again soon." They spoke in unison once again.

"Likewise," I said as Poppy rushed me out of the suite.

Poppy guided me to the courtyard where the ceremony was to be held. My stomach tightened as I saw the rows of people sitting and waiting for me. To my surprise, the end of the aisle was empty. No Ezra or priestess in sight.

"There is one place I need to take you before the ceremony starts," Poppy said in a hushed tone. She guided me to a nearby study, where Ezra was pacing back and forth. There was a desk, which was covered with papers, and a shelf full of old books. Only half the sconces were lit, giving the room dim lighting. This was not where I expected to see Ezra just before our wedding. I did not think he could look any more handsome than he already did, but he proved me wrong. His long white hair was in a neat top knot. His suit matched the color of his wings, pure black with golden embellishments.

What shocked me was the human woman in purple robes. She had the seamstress's face. How was this possible? The seamstress was fae, but the woman now standing in front of me was wingless and with rounded ears. She gave me a warm smile.

"Ah, so you truly did not know who I was. Good, I was worried your answers were based on your knowledge of my intentions."

"What do you mean?" I questioned.

Ezra stopped pacing and snapped his gaze toward me. "You already spoke to Amara? How dare you!" His face contorted with rage.

"Hush boy," she snapped. "Yes, I did not want your influence on her. I wanted to see how she truly felt about you."

"And what did she say?!" He looked down at her nervously.

"Don't talk about me like I am not here! Can someone explain to me what is going on?" I shouted at them.

Ezra's gaze lowered. "I am sorry." He spoke in a quiet tone as he walked over to my side, taking my hands into his.

The woman glared at us. "My true name is Elara Mazzeo. I am the one who enacted the curse all those centuries ago."

My jaw fell slack. She looked to be in her early forties. I could not imagine her being centuries old.

"I apologize for deceiving you," she continued. "I needed to test your true feelings for the king. While Ezra is truly different from the kings who came before him, I still had to see if a woman with a stone heart who hated the fae could love a fae king."

My body tensed, and Ezra wrapped his arm around me, holding me close.

"Luckily for him, you truly do care. I will end the curse, under one condition." A dubious grin crossed her face.

"Enough of your conditions, witch! We have already met your original terms. End this, now!"

She took a step closer. Everything in my body screamed at me to run. I could sense the overwhelming power she had. Feeling it now, I do not know how I did not before.

"Seeing I am the game master and you are my pawns, you do not have a choice."

Ezra's shadows surrounded us, and my nerves eased. There was something about him that gave me an over-whelming sense of protection.

She circled us for a moment, looking at us up and down. Stopping in front of us, she placed her hand on her chin, rubbing it as she continued to stare us down. "I will end the curse if you agree to never see each other ever again." Her voice was cold.

The calmness Ezra provided was now gone. That feel-ing was now taken over by a stabbing feeling in my chest. He held me tighter to him. Tears welled in my eyes at her words.

"No!" We both cried out.

"No? Do you want your people to continue to turn into monsters? Would you choose a human woman you just met over your people?"

"Please," Ezra begged. His voice shook as he spoke. "Do not make me choose. I want to save my people, but I can't imagine a world without Amara. For centuries, I lived in the dark, content with lurking in the shadows. Now that I have seen the sun, and felt its warmth on my skin, I cannot return to the darkness."

Elara rolled her eyes and then her dark gaze fell on me. "How do you feel about that?"

"I don't want to leave him. Ezra has shown me a world I did not know I needed. For my entire life, I expected to be alone. Now, I could not imagine my life without him. I love him!"

Ezra smiled down at me, and gently ran the back of his fingers across my cheek. "I love you, too," he said softly.

"You have proven me wrong. I never believed humans and fae could fall in love. So, I bound the two of you together. A human who feared the fae and a fae who hated humans. But, here you are. Truly in love with one another." Elara smirked and purple energy surrounded her. She raised her arms, palms up. The ground quaked. "From this day forth, the curse is over. All fae lost to the vox shall return. May King Ezra and Queen Amara live long and prosper!"

She chanted in a language I did not recognize. The earth quaked harder. In an explosion of purple energy, she vanished, and the earth calmed.

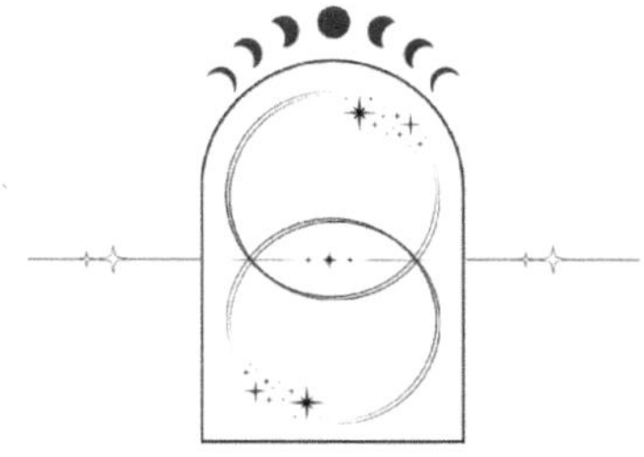

Twenty

Chaos erupted from outside the study. Ezra rushed to the door, telling Poppy and I to stay back. He yanked the door open, and the hall was full of people, running and screaming. Ezra rushed into the hallway and the crowd.

Poppy and I looked at each other. Her brow furrowed with worry. Without speaking, the two of us knew exactly what we needed to do. We both quickly rushed out of the room and into the hallway.

People were hugging and sobbing. Gil held a small woman with golden skin, hair as black as night, and wings of pure white.

"Mother above," Poppy whispered. "That is Gil's wife. She was turned into a vox many years ago. How..." she trailed off, unable to finish her question. It seemed that all fae who were transformed into vox, now somehow magically appeared in the castle.

Looking around, I saw so many reunions happening around us. Mothers who lost their children. Husbands and wives who lost each other. Fae from the other realms stood in shock as they watched the chaos unfold.

Poppy and I weaved through the crowd to try to find Ezra. I called out for him, but I was drowned out by the voices that filled the hall.

When we finally found him, a woman with white hair was sobbing into his chest. I could hear her screams and sobs over the commotion. "My baby boy! You did it!" She pulled her face away from his chest, and my heart skipped a beat as I looked at the most beautiful woman I had ever seen. She had similar angular features Ezra did, and even had the same two braids with tiny golden hoops woven in that framed her face. Her metallic silver wings were tucked neatly behind her.

A man approached them, shadows clung to him, and I swore his hair was created by those shadows. Even Ezra's shadows seemed to gravitate toward the man. His ice-blue eyes met mine, and a chill went down my spine when I saw a moon on his third eye, identical to Ezra's. The woman turned and saw the man step out of the crowd. She released Ezra and rushed to him. They held each other in a tight embrace.

His wings wrapped around them, isolating them from the chaos. His wings were as black as the void, with golden flecks throughout, they too were identical to Ezra's. I swore there were larger flecks that almost matched the tapestry from the dining room.

"Momma? Daddy?" A young girl's voice shrieked. She rushed out of the crowd. Her long dark curls flowed in the space behind her as she ran toward the man and woman. She had the same emerald eyes and metallic wings as the woman.

"Olivia," Ezra spoke in a broken tone as his gaze snapped to her, and he rushed to her, fell to his knees, and wrapped her in his arms.

"Big brother," she sobbed back, hugging him tightly.

The man and woman, who I now understood to be Ezra's parents, released each other and turned toward their children. His father's gaze fell on Poppy and me, and Poppy immediately fell to her knees and bowed her head.

"Rise," his voice was deep and smooth, just like Ezra's. "Today is a day of reconnecting and celebration. No need for formalities."

Ezra stood and walked over to me, wrapping his arm around me. "Mother, father. Let me introduce you to Amara, the human who saved us all."

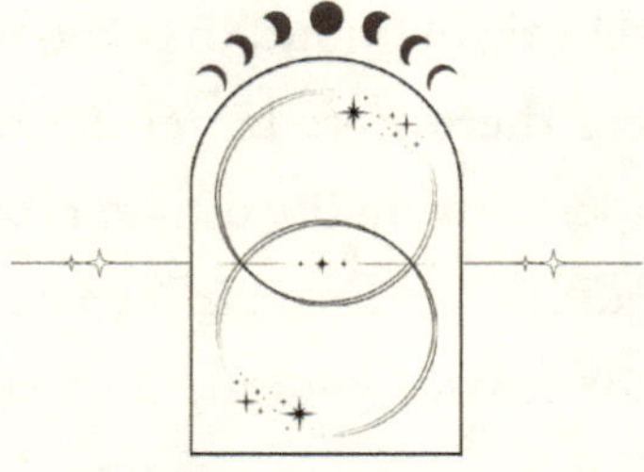

Twenty-One

"Amara!" Glenda shrieked as I stepped into the apothecary. She ran over to me and embraced me tightly. "You returned from the capital!" I held her back, trying to hold in my tears. My body quivered. I truly believed I was never going to see her again. "And who is this handsome gentleman you brought with you?" She released me and looked up at Ezra.

He had glamoured himself to look human. I was not used to his rounded ears or his lack of wings. I looked up at him and smiled, then back to Glenda. "I would like to introduce you to Ezra. I met him during my travels."

"It is great to meet you. I have heard so many good things," Ezra said softly.

Glenda rushed to the door, flipped the sign to 'closed,' and locked the door. "It is very lovely to meet you," she giggled. "Amara has never brought home a man, let alone someone so handsome. Please let's go upstairs and chat over tea! I want to hear everything about your journey!" She skipped across the room and up the stairs into the main house.

I looked up at Ezra and whispered, "I told you she would be like this."

"I think it's charming," he whispered back.

We followed her up the stairs, where she had on a kettle and taken down three mugs from the cabinet. "I hope you enjoy tea!" Glenda said as she prepared the botanicals.

"Indeed, I do." He responded as we sat down at the kitchen table. I watched him nervously and wondered what he thought of our small, modest home. "Glenda, I actually came to ask you something very important."

"Oh?" She rushed over to the table with worry in her eyes.

"Would you allow me the honor of courting Amara?" He asked in a nervous tone.

"Court? Oh my, you are truly an old-fashioned gentleman! Amara, where did you find such a catch?" She looked over to Ezra, a wide smile on her face. "I think I may like you!"

"Thank you, Glenda. I am glad to hear I made a good first impression." He chuckled nervously and shot me a grin.

"Oh, gods," I sighed. "Enough of that! Do not let his ego grow any bigger!" A laugh escaped my lips.

The kettle whistled and Glenda finished making the tea. "Amara, I already put three sugar cubes in yours. Ezra, would you like some?"

"No thank you. I enjoy the true taste of the herbs."

"Gods, you're perfect," she chuckled in response and brought us our mugs. "Jade is going to be so happy you are home! She has been here every day asking if you have returned."

"And I can't wait to see her. I have many books I need her to read. I found so many new ones during my journey!"

"Ah yes! Tell me, how was the trip? How was the capital?"

I told her the story Ezra and I practiced for the past two days. How the journey was easy, how I met Ezra in the town of Magla, and he offered to escort me to the capital and back. We informed my aunt that our client in the capital had already placed a new order with us, and would need it quickly, so I could not stay long.

Before we arrived, we talked about how we would handle telling everything to Glenda. I understood telling her I was in love with a fae king probably would not go over well.

The plan was to first make her love him just as much as I, then slowly introduce her to the truth of who he is and where I actually went while I was gone.

For now, he would glamour her into thinking I traveled to the capital often to trade herbs, salves, and other goods from our apothecary. Ezra would continue to provide me with gold to make it seem real, and to ensure my aunt would not struggle in my absence.

"I will miss you so much. Promise me you will stay safe on your travels?" Glenda's eyes misted.

"I promise. I will only be gone for a few weeks. I will be very safe."

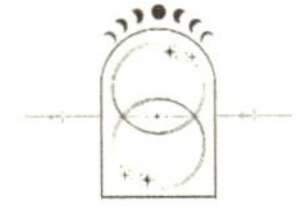

"Amara, I want to thank you officially for saving our kingdom," Julian, Ezra's father, raised his glass in a toast.

Ezra's mother, Lilianna, raised her glass as well. "Yes, and we also want to thank you for saving our son."

For the first time, the royal family all gathered for dinner after their return. Ezra still sat at the head of the table, and his father sat directly across from him, in the seat I once took. I now sat to Ezra's right. It felt so right being by his side.

"I am the King of Orilon. I do not need to be taken care of," Ezra sneered, sipping his wine.

"Big brother, you *definitely* need to be taken care of!" Princess Olivia threw her head back and laughed. She truly was such a sweet young girl. My heart broke at how young she was. When the curse claimed her, she was just a teenager.

"I am glad we were able to break the curse. I am excited to explore Orilon now that all the fae are free from their cursed forms, and it is safe again."

"It is not fully safe yet. Not until we find Elara. We won't let her get away with what she has done," Ezra snarled.

"I will be leading the hunt. You will stay here, reign over Orilon, and restore it to its former glory."

"Yes, father." Ezra nodded toward his father.

"I can't wait to get to know you better, Amara! Ezra has not stopped speaking of you since our return!" Liliana smiled at me. She had a genuine sense of kindness radiating from her.

"What is the plan now the curse is broken? Now that you don't have to be married," Olivia asked.

Ezra cleared his throat. "I am going to start from the beginning with Amara. We did not have the best start to our relationship." His gaze turned toward me. "I know I already asked your aunt, but I never asked you. Will you allow me to court you?"

Heat rose to my cheeks. "Yes!" I answered without hesitation.

"Wonderful!" He leaned in and brushed his lips against mine. Too quickly, he pulled away. "I can't wait to see where this road leads us."

"Cheers to that!" His mother raised her glass once again.

"Cheers!" The rest of us said in unison as we raised our glasses.

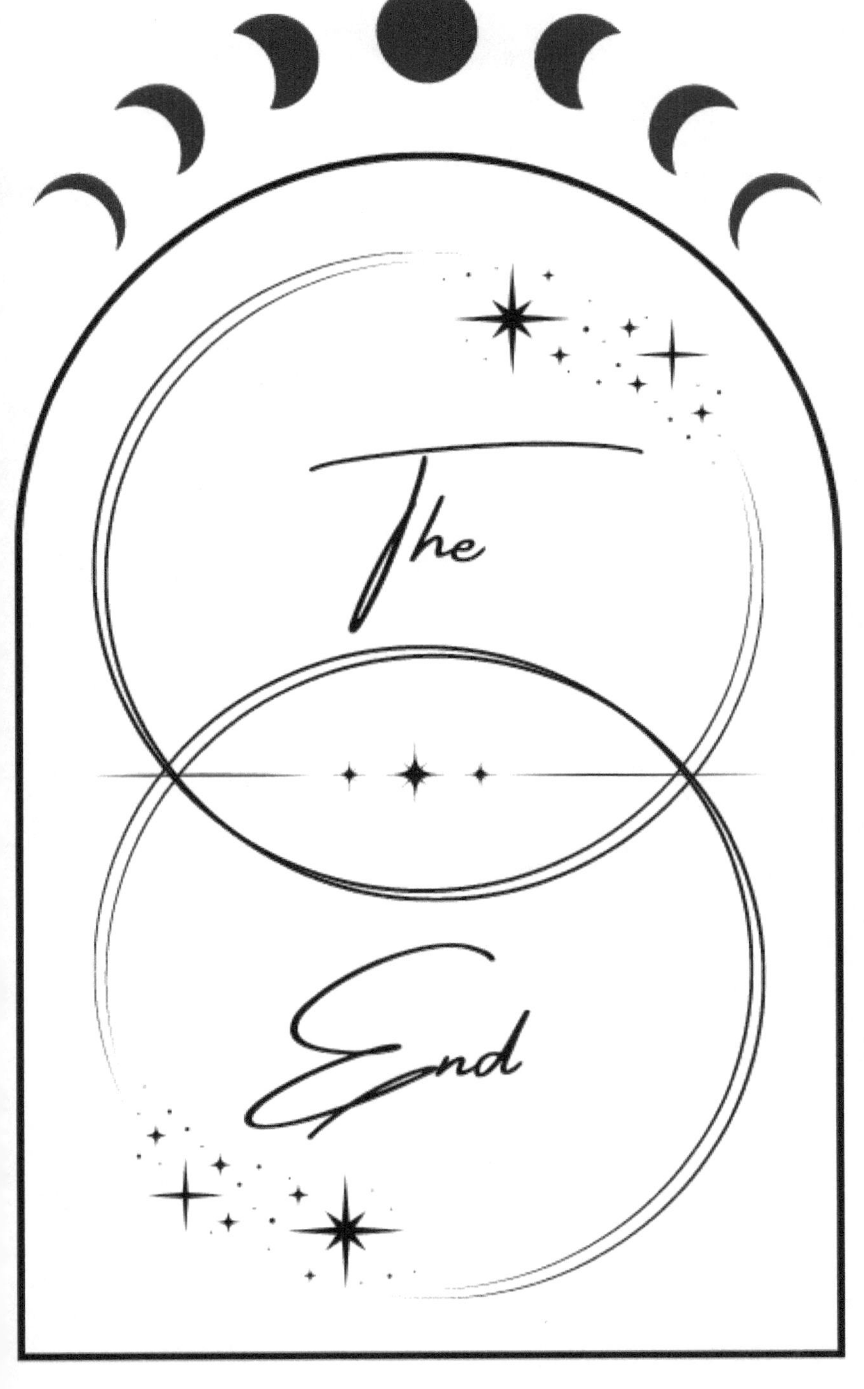
The
End

Also by Willow Asteria

The Blood Singer Trilogy
https://amzn.to/3KO4erc

The Realms of Elswyth
https://amzn.to/3xsvM2r

Learn More Here!